Grumpy Middle Aged Dad - Intercontinental Adventures

Michael Hadley

Grumpy Middle-Aged Dad– Adventures Across the World

Copyright © Michael Hadley, November 2022

Michael Hadley asserts the moral right to be identified as the author of this book.

From the Author: -

I have tried to recreate events, locales and conversations from my memories of them. In order to maintain their anonymity in some instances I have changed the names of individuals and places, I may have changed some identifying characteristics and details such as physical properties, occupations and places of residence.

Any names or characters, businesses or places, events or incidents, are fictitious.

As you will see if you manage to get to the end.

Any resemblance to actual persons, living or dead, or actual events is purely coincidental and a result of way too much gin.

All profits from this book were donated to charity. I did not make a single penny – what an idiot.

Could have easily bought a new fishing rod.

If you have reason to be offended, please don't sue me.

Michael Hadley

The Black Country, November 2022

Dedicated to Goon.

The best thing that ever happened to me.

Oh, and you were right. I am only funny on paper.

5 star Amazon reviews for The Grumpy Middle-Aged Dad – Adventures in Orlando

"What a fabulous book! I had tears rolling down my face from start to finish. One of the funniest things I have ever read! Do yourself a favour and pick up a copy – you won't be disappointed!" – L M Kimberley

"One of the funniest books I've ever read and I can relate to nearly everything in it." – Peter Harper

"Absolutely loved this book! Was a great read and definitely loads of lol moments!!" – Melissa Folkes

"Hilariously accurate… especially holidaying with teenagers. I cried with laughter. This is a man who adores his family. I can't wait for the next book." – Kay Steven

"Dad, you're not even funny." – Lottie

"Read this whilst on the train to London. People were looking at this crazy woman who was laughing out loud and just couldn't stop. That was me. A lovely funny read." –Vonnydee

"Loved it!! It was so funny from start to end!! Read in one day as I couldn't put it down." – kimmy

"I bought this as a present for my Dad for Father's Day as we have been to Orlando many times and my dad would sometimes be a bit grumpy! After giving it to him, he read it within two days and was in stitches especially as he found it so relatable. Now the whole family want to read it." – KPollak

"Great book. Laugh out loud funny for anyone who has trudged the paving stones around Disneyworld. This book reminded me so much of our family trips and I think we can all be Mr / Mrs Grumpy sometimes. Well worth a read." – Lindsay

"Absolutely excellent read, totally relatable, proper laugh out loud funny" – Amanda Mansfield-Clark

"Funniest book I've read in ages!! I enjoyed it so much read it in one sitting" – pf watson

"Can you hurry up and finish this sodding book as you're getting on my nerves now" – Missus H

"Highly entertaining read!! Definitely the book to leave in the bathroom for ALL to enjoy. Combination of Disney magic and grumpy British humour = Fantastic". – Jade

"I haven't made any of these reviews up. Honest" – Me

"I followed with interest the Grumpy Middle-Aged Dad's adventures around Orlando in his blogs, so when these were turned into a book I just had to read it. The book is both heart-warming and laugh-out-funny and clearly written with much love. Michael Hadley is a very funny man and a gifted writer" – Amanda Graham

"Read the blogs daily and they were hilarious – bought the book and had a sore face from laughing so much!! If you have ever been to Disney world or even if you haven't this is the funniest best description of the place!! 5 stars Mr Hadley, a fantastic read!!" – GLB

"I have just finished reading the antics of Grumpy & want to ask when's the next book out? I feel like I've been on the holiday with The Fam & experienced all that they have. I happen to know Grumpy & can say how proud I am of him & this truly hilarious read, in fact I wish they'd stayed for longer just so I could read more! The level of description easily transports you there (alongside Grumpy in the laundry room) for that I LOL. I got some looks at work, chuckling away to myself...so what if I should have actually been working!
So Grump, pull ya finger out ar kid & get writing the next one!" – A Black Country Lass

"Love love love! So funny, anyone who's been to Orlando can relate to Grumpy's musings. Lighthearted and fun and raising money for 2 great causes. Highly recommended!" - Jacqui L.

"A must read for all Disney and Orlando fans everywhere. This will make you laugh out loud. For those of you who think Disney is a waste of money and 'not for you' then you too will enjoy the tongue in cheek reviews!" – Helen Ellis

5 star Amazon reviews for The Grumpy Middle-Aged Dad and Lottie – More Adventures in Orlando

"These books are brilliant not only because they are funny. But a great insight to what it's like for dad's holidays in Orlando" – Roy Twiggs

"What a fantastic read!! It was hilarious, informative and self-deprecating, noting 'todays look is: Action Man!' Courtesy a plethora of local stores that we all know and love.
The book had it all, fun, sun, gin, grumpiness, love and was a very heart-warming read that made me laugh and cry in equal measure. What a feat to achieve!! Well done that man and fam!!"
– Lisa M

"I laughed and cried in equal measures. I was a top fan of the first book but life has passed me by and I've only just got round to ordering in true Disney style Part 2! I look forward to many more sequels of these utterly brilliant, funny and inspiring adventures...Not only a funny guy , compassionate, kind Michael is clearly a top dad :).” – Sara Jane

“This is an adventure of a father and daughter on holiday and is funny, poignant and full of love. Laugh out loud and cry in turn and realise how precious life is. And what a prat middle aged men can be!” – Feesa 523

“Lovely, heart-warming recount with many funny moments. Definitely worth a read and proceeds to a well-deserved charity. If you love Orlando, you will love this book!” – Maxine

“Absolutely hilarious! Michael writes from the heart about the place closest to our hearts. His sideways glance at Orlando and the bond between him and his beautiful Lottie is a joy to read”. – Valerie Tucker

“Why didn’t you write a book about me, Dad?” – Sam

“Grumpy is back!! Anyone who's a fan of Florida, the happy place known as Disney, any other parks or just needs a smile in their lives needs this book and the first one too. It is impossible to read them without laughing out loud, they are just brilliant. Thanks, Michael, for the laughs, can't wait for the next one now.... no pressure! Oh yes, and it raises lots of £££ for charity, win win all round!” – Sally

"Loving these books, my eldest read some and had a chuckle then I read some to our 4 year old both said "sounds just like dad". We love Florida and these are great reads for plane journey or before you go. Even better that the money made goes to charity. Well done Michael and family" – Iona

"Mr Grumpy's second and no less impressive book on his adventures in Florida. No second book sequel worries here, if anything it's better, having more "tug at the heart string" moments to enjoy.

If you have never been to Florida for a family holiday then this is a must read. It's not a travel guide or idealistic view of the sunshine state, this is a raw 'experience it first hand' account of a dad and his daughter on holiday. You will learn lots to help you make the best of your Florida holiday, and perhaps realise that what's important is the family time together and not if you got a fast pass for Avatar or not.

Enjoy". – Timothy T

"What a beautiful, heart-warming, funny journey to be taken on when reading this book. Michael transports you to the most treasured and scary times in his life with his quick witted and descriptive writing. Laugh out loud is a must when reading this book. Shedding a tear or two is optional (as is growing up :)) Lottie's witty words are the cherry on the cake.

Makes me want to go back to Orlando sooner rather than later. Happy reading". – Stacey G

Facebook reviews for the Disneyland Paris blogs

(I highly recommend Disneyland Paris Info Zone, Disneyland Paris chat for Brits and Disneyland Paris Tips for Brits if you're going to Disneyland Paris – they're ace)

"Your post is brilliant - informative and funny - I wouldn't expect anything less" – A Coleman

"Hello. I read you every day from Belgium. I also know the park. He is fantastic. Thank you for making us dream again" – Agnes from Belgium

"You're a legend, loving your posts" – S Longley

"This style of blog doesn't really work in our group – we love clear and helpful trip reports without double entendre and bad jokes which aren't necessary in a group with small eyes watching" – Faceless, Nameless, Mood Hoover from Disneyland Paris For Brits

"Been looking forward to reading your blog entry today! We left today after 4 incredible days and reading your adventures definitely help me get over the blues of heading home" – Michelle H

"I'm in Wetherspoons crying with laughter... actually spat my brew out laughing at one point and now all the locals are staring at me" – Emma D

"Your posts have been amazing; I've loved reading them! I couldn't breathe for laughing! So glad you've had such a lovely holiday, Disney really is magic x". – Sarah S

"Love love LOVE these posts and yes I cried too at this one. Can't wait to take my 3 year old for his 3rd DLP trip next month. Disney memories with little ones are the absolute best!" – Aimee S

"My babies are 9 and 5. And I already feel like they're growing so fast. I love these posts". – Chris De-C

"Absolutely love reading your posts, making me so much more excited for our first trip in December x" – Emma C

"Love your posts! This one has had me laughing and filling up making me more excited for my family trip next year!" – Nicole B

"Thanks for your blog, I love your humour" – Helen L

"Literally crying. I'm going for the first time next year, my kids will be 8 and 5 and I'll remind myself to soak up every minute" – Stacey H

"Best review ever, thanks for making me laugh!" – Alison B

"Oh my, can you add a warning please… I was happily reading your well written funny post and

then you hit us with an emotional wrecking ball!"
– Sidney M

"I was chuckling away, and then I got to the end
and immediately wanted to wake my daughter
up so I can hug her" – Kate H

"Really funny, and then bam, you made me cry!
You should be a writer (if you aren't already!)" –
Jo P

"You've got such a way with words, loving your
posts x". – Nicola E

Reviews of Michael Hadley as a person

"He makes me feel special" – Missus H

"He's a very careful driver" – Sam

"As a Dad he's ok but he chews too loud" - Lottie

"He's still got his own teeth" – Mum

Grumpy Middle-Aged Dad – Intercontinental Adventures

Contents

First of all, an apology to all you pedanticks out there who like to see page numbers in the right order, starting from a logical place in the book. I have no idea how to do that so after about 28 attempts I gave up and that's why the "Contents" is page number 1.

Also, I have no clue how to do page breaks – that's why some chapters start on the left, some on the right. After 85 goes and a bottle of Yellow Tail trying to sort that out, I eventually let out a pitiful "I can't do this anymore…", cried into a Kinder Bueno and gave up.

I did try to call Jeff Bezos so he could talk me through this poxy Amazon self-publishing lark but he was out, apparently.

Probably flying a satellite somewhere.

Prick.

Anyway, it sort of looks like a book so just crack on.

Here's the contents, which are 95% accurate but don't have page numbers. Just flick through for yourself…

Acknowledgements

When I stop and look back to the start of this Orlando / Disney madness, it still amazes me that this all actually happened. I went from dicking about, writing a few bad jokes on Facebook to fulfilling a lifelong ambition to write a book. Now three books.

It's proper mad.

The success of the first two books still blows my mind (combined sales in excess of 2,500 and more than £20k raised for charity). My ego was massaged so much that I ended up doing a bit of stand-up comedy and writing loads more for other projects. I also had the privilege to be involved with the charity, Meningitis Now.

I've met some amazing people along the way and had some truly incredible (life changing, even) experiences. I've been blessed with so much love, support and encouragement from all of them, and I am lucky beyond words that they are in my life.

If you bought one or both of my books, and you are now obviously in possession of my third one, I cannot thank you enough. Your support means so much to me and I thank you from the bottom of my heart. If, on the other hand, you have not read either of the first two, I urge you to give them a go before they end up pulped.

Oh, and Amazon loves a five-star review on my books so be a mate and pop one on for me. Jeff Bezos plants a tree, releases a Discovery Cove dolphin back into the wild and personally donates $500.00 to charity each time I get one. *

It is my absolute honour and privilege to give extra special mentions to the following wonderful people who went above and beyond in helping to make this book a reality.

Peter Harper and Tony Fullam from *Orlando Info Zone* and *It's Orlando Time* - two amazing Facebook sites packed with great info and lovely people and where I posted all the original blogs. Both are top blokes and allowed me the self-indulgent publicity to promote all three books.

An extra nod to the *Disneyland Paris* and *Orlando Info Zone* admin teams too, who are a wonderful group of people who have also shown me great support – I was proud to be part of the OIZ team for a short while and your collective loveliness has helped me enormously.

Thank you to the teams from the two nominated charities who will receive **all** the profits from this book.

Meningitis Now is my chosen charity – my daughter Lottie contracted meningitis at just 4 weeks old. Her life was saved by gang of real-life superhero doctors and nurses, and I will be forever grateful. She's now a superhero herself, saving lives as a Paramedic – that would never have been possible without the skill, dedication and expertise provided by the incredible people in the NHS, who in turn are supported by thousands of incredible charities all across the country. Meningitis Now is one of the most incredibleist of them all.

The Dudley Leukaemia Unit Appeal Fund was nominated by my Black Country mate and fellow Orlando nerd, Paul Elwell. Paul lost his father Jack to leukaemia in September 2020, and he told me how touched he was by the care and support they gave to him and the family to help cope with his loss. They are an incredible bunch of people, providing much needed care to patients and relatives in their time of need.

That brings me neatly to the two forewords... the aforementioned Paul Elwell is an Orlando Facebook legend and along with his own Missus E, Jo, spend as much time over there as possible. His knowledge of Orlando is second to none and he's given advice and help to countless thousands of people for their own holidays over in the sunshine state. There's no doubt that Paul has changed lives with his guidance and support through the Facebook group *It's Orlando Time*, helping people wherever he can to make sure they get the most out of their holiday. He also shares my love of everything Black Country, especially scratchings.

Kath Watson is another Orlando superstar and quite possibly the nicest person I have ever had the privilege to meet. Along with hubby Bob and kids Becky and Charlie, she's also an Orlando nutjob and helps with the admin on the Orlando Facebook groups, *It's Orlando Time* and *Orlando Info Zone*. You know when you meet someone, and they leave a long-lasting impression on you? When that person is radiant, helpful, kind, happy, supportive and just a generally wonderful human being? Well, that's Kath Watson. She should be prescribed on the NHS to cheer people up.

I am humbled that both these beautiful souls took time to write nice thigs about me and the books. Ta.

Thanks to Amanda Coleman, proof-reader extraordinaire who corrected my grammar and helped to construct it into a book n that, along with Amanda Stedman who is a trusted source of information and guidance and is never shy in pointing out that I'm not as funny as she is. As before, my mega talented and super mum-in-law Ruth Cleeton also used her skills to help with spell chcking. Ruth's helped me out on all three books now and I am eternally grateful. The very talented Ian Stroud of Charles Design, Kingswinford helped with touching up the front cover – top bloke and did it for nowt.

What a team.

I'm indebted to all of my wonderful work colleagues at the car spares mine in Brierley Hill. My team left me alone to invent all this nonsense while they carried on working hard to keep the business going. In particular I'd like to thank Joy, Jason, Julian, Heather, Daz and Dan – you're all fab and I think the world of you. You still have to buy a book though.

Also thanks to my long time business partner, cousin / uncle Big Willy Hadley for putting up with me pissing off for six weeks.

Special belly rubs to the three little bundles of love, energy and mischief who have collectively turned our little Black Country cottage into a kennel. Molly, Pip and Rosie obviously can't read but Missus H made me include them. Woof.

Thanks to my mum and dad for bringing me up in the harsh world of the Black Country which unwittingly provided umpteen anecdotes and tons of material. I will be forever grateful for your love, help and support and you're both at the beating heart of everything I've ever done and achieved.

To Sam and Lottie, my two beautiful kids. I could not be any more proud of both of you and I love you dearly. I'm astonished on a daily basis that I helped create two amazing, talented, wonderful human beings. You two are the best of me.

Finally, to my dear Catherine. None of this happens without you. I'm beyond gratitude for everything you've ever done for me and the love and support I get every day. I have no idea how an incredible human like you has tolerated a bozo like me for so long.

I love you with all of my heart.

(* - this may or may not be true. Probably isn't.)

Foreword by Paul Elwell

In July 2022, I received a message off Michael, asking for me to undertake the forward to his upcoming best seller, 3rd edition book of his travels abroad.

Some may know me, as I am Tony Fullam's (no 1), and admin for the Facebook Group, It's Orlando Time. I often chuckle when Tony refers to me as his no 1....I'd say I'm more of a no 2 personally.

Jo (my Missus E) and I have been going to Orlando for almost 30 years and have 30 odd stickers on the side of the plane, and we both still learn facts and "things to do" both from IOT and The adventures of Michael. Not only have they helped us, but also many members of the group, and hats off, cause both those members have thanked Michael personally.

IOT as it's known, deals with all aspects of trips, experience's and even which toilets are the best at each park....this is how I got the pleasure of meeting Michael, not through our love of toilets, but the passion that is It's Orlando Time. Jo and I have had the pleasure of meeting Michael, and his good wife and family a few times, including the carvery counter at The Dudley Arms, the back of Heron Foods in Kingswinford, underneath the Tree of Shite, and even in the place we all call home, Orlando.

Michaels use of words and being a fellow Black Country Chap, has made his previous books fly off the shelf and offer "an alternative" spin on Orlando but at the same time, amusing but extremely informative, in the way Michael knows best.

The latest addition deals again with Michaels views of Orlando and covers previous trips to Disney in California, Orlando and Paris. I am sure that we will all gain more benefit and have even bigger belly chuckles to his trials and tribulations overseas.

I'd like to finish this foreword by thanking Michael for all his efforts in donating any profits from previous books, and indeed this one, to charity. I believe Michael has raised over £20,000 previously and I expect that to rise.

An even bigger honour was Michael asking me which charity Jo and I would like on this book.... well back in Sept 2020, I lost my father to Leukaemia, and that is very close to my heart as well so I've suggest the Leukaemia Trust at Russell's Hall Hospital.

Enjoy the book folks and let's all give our thanks to Michael for another fab read.

Tara a bit

Paul x

Foreword by Kath Watson

I first discovered Michael through his blogs on the Facebook group, It's Orlando Time. Each morning I would eagerly open the page and laugh out loud at his sideways and sometimes irreverent chronicles of holidaying in Orlando.

He affectionately describes himself as "Grumpy" but he leaves his readers in no doubt that he is, in fact, a gentle, gin soaked, jolly sort of chap. He delights in finding joy in each day, in sharing his memoirs and making us convulse into hysterics one minute and reaching for a tissue to wipe away tears the next. His love for his wife Catherine and his children Sam and Lottie is evidcnt in his writing and after meeting them, you can see why.

His first book grabbed readers by their funny bone and didn't let go until their sides hurt. His second book did not disappoint as he returned to Orlando with Lottie and we chuckled along with their adventures and delighted in their father/daughter fun. I made the mistake of reading the book in the garden and startled the neighbours with my screams and howls of uncontrollable laughter.

The whole world has missed out on much fun and laughter these past few years and this latest book promises to redress the balance. If you want to belly laugh as the empty nesters romp around some of the world's iconic Disney theme parks you will not be disappointed. You have picked up a book you won't be able to put down unless it's to gasp for breath or choke back a tear.

His excitement and passion for Disney is shared with his audience in addition to the many hints and tips for getting the most out of your trip. He shares his exploits with much humour and makes us giggle and cry at his observations and saucy punchlines. He stirs a myriad of emotions as he recalls holidaying when his children were small and we smile and nod in agreement. His writing leaves us with a sense of happy satisfaction and enjoyment and leaves us with a warm and fuzzy feeling, a real boost to our well-being.

Michael brings his original and unique perspective to a topic that is so well documented by so many authors, bloggers and vloggers all over the world and his distinctive authentic style makes it instantly engaging.

He is a kind and generous friend and I am privileged and proud to know him. Through Michael's work I have been inspired in my own writing and I am indebted for his support and guidance with the Live events we hosted together on the Facebook group Orlando Info Zone.

Pssssttt….

Pssssttt….

Oi!!

You!!

Yes, **you**. The one who's reading this.

Well, who else would I be talking to?

I'm Michael. I wrote this book, the one that you're holding in your hands.

I'm in your head now.

For reference, my accent is sort of singy songy, slightly camp, Black Country – for those that don't know imagine a slightly happier Brummie accent with rounder soft edges.

Hello!!

(Imagine me waving. Waving back is strongly encouraged but optional)

I'm sat in my kitchen writing this bit first, before the book has even been started as I've got something quite important to tell you.

This is just between me and you, though, right?

(I'm beckoning you closer to whisper in your ear as I lower my voice into a sexy, husky whisper and say...)

No-one else is ever going to have this moment...

Ever...

This first, shared moment between the two of us. This unique bond between you, the reader and me, the author.

It's totally unique. A one-off. The only one of its kind.

Like Kylie.

Reading a book truly is a solitary pastime. Unless you are a conjoined twin, in which case you may have two books and read them simultaneously. Or one book and one of you reads to the other head. I suppose you could take it in turns.

But mainly reading is done alone, and the bond between reader and writer is wondrously, extraordinarily, uniquely special and only exists in your head.

Or heads.

Can't stop thinking of conjoined twins now. If you are one and you need two books, get in touch for a discount on a bulk buy.

By this point you have already created my voice, characterised my accent and started to form an impression of the kinda guy I am. If you don't know what I look like, don't Google me just yet but instead picture a ruggedly handsome, slightly weathered bloke with piercing blue eyes and a full head of luscious sandy blonde hair. And less than 5% body fat, an IQ to rival Stephen Fry and a penis the size of a Pringles tube.

If you like what you've read so far, lean in and I'll let you into another secret.

Everyone, and I do mean <u>everyone</u>, other than me and you, is stupid.

Everyone outside this wondrous little bubble that you and I have created in just a few paragraphs is as thick as mince. I don't mean Joey Essex stupid; I mean more like "they'll never really understand this bond that we have" kinda stupid.

They won't "get" it so let's not bother trying and instead keep this new, blossoming romance to ourselves; settle back, relax and just enjoy each other's company for a while. And, hey, I don't discriminate – you'll find this book is totally PC and I don't mind if you're a hot sexy chick, a girl who thinks he's a fish or a poofta. You're all the same to me.

Whoever / whatever you are, you do the reading and I'll do the entertaining. Place your trust in me and my warped imagination and I'll take you on a comedy journey filled with giggles, belly laughs, tall stories and bad jokes. After painting scenes of pre-departure domestic bliss in the Black Country, let me shuffle you through airports, fly you high above the turbulence and transfer you to your destination. We're going to boot scoot through Disneyland California, boogie on down to the psycho parks in Orlando and end our literary journey in the chic surroundings of Disneyland Paris.

This book is the extended version of the original blogs that appeared across various Orlando and Disney related Facebook sites but contains all the extra adult material, funny bits, rude jokes and swearing that I wasn't allowed to do unless I wanted to get banned by Mark Zuckerberg.

If you have bought this book expecting some sort of "travel guide" type affair, then I'm afraid you may well be disappointed. Although it does contain a few tips, tricks and travel hacks, mainly about petty theft from airport lounges and hotels, this is not the sort of material that Tim Trackit would put his name to.

However, I would encourage you to plough on nonetheless. After all, you've got this far, you've paid your money and I'm in your head now.

The book acts as a record of the dafter, more obscure things and my daily rants are a sideways look at the hot madness that is Disney and

Orlando, across the various parks I've visited on two different continents. I'd like to think that I offer a different yet highly realistic, no holds barred, warts and all perspective of the holiday that everyone is REALLY having, and not the one you imagined before you went or relayed to your friends for weeks and months after.

This is in stark contrast to many, many other online blogs that paint a happy picture of a perfect holiday where nothing ever seems to go wrong – where you don't get the shits, where you don't row with the kids and don't bristle every time you realise that there's an extra 20% added to your bill to cover the cost of the staff just to do the job they're already getting paid for.

In this pretend Disney it's all sweetness and light, with daily blogged updates on great meals, fab weather and well-behaved kids.

But what we all really know is that it's too hot, too expensive, your feet hurt A LOT and every day is a costly, tortuous, mind frazzling miserable grind to make sure that every member of the family is happy and having a Magical time - which they ought to be the ungrateful little sods as you've spent more money getting here than you did on your first four cars.

So, my new best friend, find yourself a bit of peace and quiet, shut out the stupid people in your life, grab a glass of wine in one hand and my virtual hand in the other and join me as we embark on this unique journey together...

Michael Hadley

Aged 54

Mousekeeping

Just a bit of tidying up to do before we go any further so you get the gist of the book and have more chance of making sense of it all.

Think of this short chapter as a bit like an IKEA instruction manual - very basic but ultimately necessary if you want your Jism chest of drawers to stand up. Hopefully you'll read this, take note and not get to the end and think "what the fuck was that all about?" - the equivalent of putting said chest of drawers in place then finding a suspicious spare nut and bolt as it collapses into a pile of knickers and cheap MDF.

Following on from the success of the first two books (over 3000 sold, more than £20 grand raised for charity... that still blows my mind...) I started this book in California on the first leg of me and Missus H's holiday back in 2019. The intention was to blog around Disneyland California and then add in the week or so we spent in the Orlando parks – all of the Disneys and a bit of Universal.

Then an Ozzy Osborne fan in China ate a bat and the World collapsed in on itself.

Subsequently, life was turned upside down for some time and it just didn't feel right to be writing about past, joyful holidays when most of us were either grieving or worrying that we could get coughed on and die.

The book was mothballed. In all honesty, I thought it would never to see the light of day.

When it was safe to come out and life started to get back to normal, I started looking through some of the Orlando Facebook pages – this inevitably led to the "Orlando itch" (not to be confused with "chub rub" which is a common ailment amongst you lovely ladies. I'm told liquid talc is the new thing to try. Or walking like you have an imaginary Shetland pony between your legs).

The "itch" usually precedes booking the next inheritance draining holiday, but travel restrictions put paid to that idea. I also had the nagging feeling that the book was still sitting on my laptop, like that expensive suit or dress you've bought but worn once and shoved back in the wardrobe. So, just like a piece of rarely worn clothing, I metaphorically got it out of the wardrobe to see if it still fitted and was still trendy.

Luckily, it did and after a few read throughs I realised that there was way too much good material in the original draft to ignore so dusted off the brain cobwebs and started again. The result is the first part of the book, covering California and Orlando.

I realised that memoirs of a past holiday in happier, pre Covid times might not have the same resonance 3 years later on so decided I needed to freshen up with a new Disney fix. Canine commitments (more of that later...) meant that any more than 6 hours out of the house was out of the question. As there isn't a Disneyland Dudley and Drayton Manor Park doesn't have anything like It's A Small World, the closest we could get was Disneyland Paris. So Missus H and I booked a trip to see Monsieur Disney à Paris – this happily coincided with the thirty year celebration of the park and 30 years of us being together.

So, there you have it. Multiple parks, in two countries on different continents, spread across 4 years with a worldwide pandemic in between.

It's either a literary masterpiece or Pluto's dinner.

Read on and decide yourself.

Enjoy.

Here we jolly well go again

I'm making a habit of these "once in a lifetime" holidays. This is the third one in a row to US, which were preceded not that many years ago by two "once in a lifetime" trips to Australia. Either the "once in a lifetime" cliché is wearing thin or I'm destined to be perpetually re-incarnated as an air steward. Given the fact that I've managed to drag pretty much the same story into three books, I suspect it's the former.

Although this is the third book, I won't assume that you read the first two (which are hilarious, by the way and still available from me or Amazon) so please allow me, dear reader, to set the scene.

I'm from the Black Country, a non-defined area of the West Midlands famous for heavy industry, coal mines and miserable people with slow, dreary accents. The Black Country accent is a bit Brummie, but a touch softer and slowed down like the speaker is simultaneously trying to say something important whilst having open brain surgery. To the outsider, the accent can be a bit strange - in our house, even Alexa shrugs.

Even the town names in the Black Country sound miserable. Not far from where I'm writing this, we've got Bilston... Tipton... Smethwick... There's a big Morrisons near us in a "village" called Moxley. This always sounds like a disease to me.

"Am yow cummin' aht ternoight aer kid?"

(*Are you coming out tonight, old chum*)

"Nah, I cor. The missus has got the moxley an we'm waerting fuh the nuss to cum rahnd..."

(*Sorry, old bean, can't make it as my dear wife has the Moxley and we await medical attention*)

To brighten up the area, clever Black Country town planners decided to have some fun with street names – hence we have Hardon Road in Wolverhampton, Mincing Lane in Blackheath and Bell End in Rowley.

Our few claims to fame are that the anchor for the Titanic was made in a Black Country town called Cradley Heath (not much use was it, that?), Sir Lenny Henry was born in Dudley and we once had a finalist in the X Factor called Wagner.

I work in a dilapidated old town called Brierley Hill. I've worked here for over 30 years, surrounded by the bleak, post-industrial wasteland and picking up on the dour, gloomy outlook of the wretched inhabitants. It goes some way to explaining why I'm such a miserable git.

If you don't know Brierley Hill, just imagine Chernobyl with a Poundland.

It has the highest concentration of vape shops in any High Street and is the only town in the UK where you can get your haircut in the middle aisle of Aldi.

It's sooo bad that even Greggs pulled out. Which is a real shame because not only did it deprive the inhabitants of one of their five-a-day (they count pastry as one of em), but every time that glass cabinet was filled full of sausage rolls, it tripled the towns IQ.

When someone eats a pork pie in Brierley Hill it <u>adds</u> to the chromosomes in the gene pool.

No wonder then that I try to get as far away from my daily reality by spending time in the insane world that is the U S of A, and specifically, Disney.

To satisfy my Disney and adrenaline addiction, I managed to persuade my long suffering and MUCH better half Catherine, henceforth known as Missus H, to accompany me on this trip – we're off to California first for a mixture of work and play, followed by a week or so in Orlando. This was on the promise that it would be the last one before we spend a quarter of my pension building that big extension on the front drive that we don't need.

We've been married for... errmmmm... ages. I don't know how long exactly but our marriage has produced two grown up kids, a house in deepest Black Country and many years of happiness.

The kids weren't born "grown up", obviously – that would be weird.

Although the eldest, Sam, was born with a cone shaped head and Lottie came out with a full head of thick black hair so both arrivals were a little strange. I was present at both births to witness these incredible moments – Sam looked like he was wearing a dunce hat and when Lottie started to squeeze out, I thought Missus H was giving birth to a Grenadier Guard.

There's just the two of us going to the States this time – Sam and Lottie, who have both played unwitting star roles in my previous holiday books, have much, much better things to do this summer like parties, festivals and life. They didn't exactly reply when asked if they wanted to come with us or spend three weeks at home, parent free, but the fact that a Facebook Event at my house titled "Hadley House Rave, bring da Giggle Smoke" immediately appeared on my timeline for the day we departed Heathrow said it all.

This was quite a sad moment for me, when they decided not to come. I confess it made this Grumpy old git a little emotional. But I realise that I can't turn back time and that they are now old enough to make their own decisions. Most notably, not to spend any time with me.

I really do wish they were coming with us.

Anyhoo, as it's just me and Missus H, we're planning on doing our own thing and seeing more of the "adult" side of Humerica.

When I say "adult" I don't mean THAT kind of adult, perverts. What I really mean is lots of alcohol and the freedom to come and go as we please - enjoy the many bars and establishments that were previously out of reach when you're with stroppy, hot, mardy kids. I've always fancied an evening boot scootin' at Margaritaville or spending a long, lazy day by the pool with a Long Island Iced Tea in one hand and Missus H's bum in the other.

Now, I'm not advocating anything seedy, although in the build up to the holiday I have been dropping subtle hints about finally being able to go to Hooters (we've been to Orlando three times now and I've yet to persuade her to go) I've been told that it's well worth a visit and does great chicken. Well, that's my story and I'm sticking to it like Bourbon Sauce on a rib.

Another welcome side effect to the kids not coming is that it shouldn't cost so much money this time – at least I won't be spending my hard-earned dollars on 3-gallon fizzy drinks you can't get your arms round and Disney tat for the hot moody kids. However, I'm already prepared to blow another Star Wars black hole in my life savings and added an extra 12 months to my retirement age (I'm gonna be 76 now) all so I can get my Disney fix.

It'd be cheaper to be addicted to pure heroin.

Missus H isn't expensive to be with on holiday. She doesn't have extravagant taste, is not that bothered about "outlet shopping" and doesn't eat a lot - she can run all day on just a slice of toast and 15 cups of tea.

In saying that, she has got a thirst for gin and does like a "mooch in the gift shop", which over the years I've come to realise is shorthand for "I'm just about to spend at least what you earn in a day on presents for those nephews you don't like". More about her in the next chapter.

As for me, I realise that I'm getting old.

There's a lot of disadvantages to getting old. I don't recommend it.

Along with the aching bones, the unexpected trumps, the hair loss (or growth, in my case, especially nostril and ear hair which seems to have developed a new lease of life altogether) and the longer than usual dribbly piddles, life comes into sharper focus and things begin to dawn on you like you've had an awakening.

I now understand that life is cruel, and that God is playing one almighty trick on all of us – especially Grumpy Middle-Aged Men. Men of my vintage are right on the tipping point of two things – we have the wisdom, experience and knowledge to tackle most of our and everyone else's problems, yet now we lack the energy, enthusiasm and stamina to be bothered to do anything about it.

I'll give you a couple of examples of just how cruel this is.

As I've got older, my memory has failed me. Names, places, events have all got lost in the fog of time, buried beneath layers of work and life related stress. But I know I've had a great time – I've met some amazing, funny people, been to incredible places and done some truly amazing things. I just can't remember them...

Also, when I was younger, thinner, fitter and much better-looking version of this jowelly old git that I am now, I knew nothing.

Absolutely nothing.

I had no common sense, no personality and nothing to say, but I did have great hair, nice clothes and a six pack. Now, with thinning hair, Primark clothes and an expanding waistline comes great wisdom - I've got confidence, knowledge, and great life stories... but no-one is interested.

I've come to realise that society is conditioned not to listen to Grumpy old gits like me.

I got a little depressed about this for a short while, so sought help from Dudley's famous psychiatric doctor, E.A. Right. Unfortunately he couldn't help me with my depression, but he did give me a thorough physical examination. Which was weird as I didn't ask for one.

I should have known it was a little strange when I went into his surgery and he said:

"Take off all your clothes and lie on the bed"

I said: "Where shall I put them?"

"On top of my mine"

Much to my surprise, he then proceeded to check me all over (and I mean ALL over). He said:

"Don't worry Mr Hadley, it's not unusual to get an erection during this type of examination".

"But I haven't got one" I replied.

"No, but I have"

Anyway, I got the big thumbs up for my prostrate so at least I don't have to worry about that.

I digress. So, the passing of time and the rise in irritability makes us Grumpies even more curmudgeonly, even more cantankerous and even harder work to be around. I get exasperated on an hourly basis, my fuse getting shorter and my triggers becoming plentiful. I get wound up at the slightest thing… more stupid people seem to creep into my life and demonstrate more brazen acts of stupidity.

I'm that petty I compiled a list:

- People who do their weekly shop or check 10 weeks worth of Lotto tickets at a Tesco Express after they've filled up with petrol and leave their car blocking a pump.
- People who can't spell properly. Specifically, people who spell "specifically" as "pacifically". And people that call you "guys" or say "from the get go". And don't get me started on idiots on social media who say "If you know, you know…"
- People who leave bags on train seats when the carriage is packed.
- People who bash into you cos they're watching films on their phones whilst walking.
- Anyone who watches Love Island.

So, there you have it, you've met me, you know where I'm from and where I work. Now it's time for you to meet Missus H.

Missus H

For better or worse, and despite being a total and utter buffoon, my marriage is still going strong after 24 years. *

Marriage happens when two people who were previously happy as individuals decide to forsake a lifetime of doing whatever they want and pledge allegiance to another human being, thus removing all sense of "self" and resigning themselves to spending weekends trudging around garden centres and repeatedly loading the dishwasher incorrectly.

After you've been married for a while, you realise that life isn't exactly as you'd planned as fresh faced youngsters, and that the dreams you both had of spending boozy weekends with mates at festivals, travelling to cosy village pubs and lazing around together on a Sunday morning drinking frothy coffee are quickly replaced by cleaning pubes out of the shower tray, rowing over who's turn it is to take the bins out and battling over Sky Plus as there's only 3% left and she wants to record all the programmes that have got Ant and Dec in them. Which is pretty much everything.

I've been married for 24 years as I write this, and in that time I've been right on 4 occasions, she's let me wear the trousers at least twice and I've successfully loaded the dishwasher correctly 3 times in a row!

** curtsies ** "I-thank-you..."

Like my male brothers, I love everything about women - the curves, the hair, the way they dress, the whiff of perfume...

Oh my god that whiff... it's like catnip for dumb men and we sniff it up in a dozy state like them kids dreamily getting a good old waft in that 1970's advert for Bisto gravy.

That's what does us. The allure of a woman sends impulses to any dopey man's brain and he would literally do anything to win her heart...

To prove his worth above all others... To show her that he's her man and the only one she needs... To sweep her off her feet and feel loved and protected...

...simply on the off chance of a quick hand job.

(I don't think Shakespeare could have written that any better)

But women are a mysterious bunch and us dopey men have really no idea what's going on.

No idea.

At. All.

For more context, let's spend a little time examining the specific heavenly woman that chose to spend her life with me, and who plays the starring role in this colourful journey first through America and then Paris, Catherine Helen Hadley, known affectionately throughout the rest of the book as Missus H.

I describe Missus H as a wonderful conundrum, beautifully packed in a little baffling box, covered in mystifying wrapping paper, tied with a puzzling bow. With a padlock on it with a big sign covered in barbed wire that says, "if you can work out what I'm thinking, I'll let ya."

She's petite at 5 foot three, has curves in <u>all</u> the right places and looks a lot like Kylie but with bigger teeth. She has an addiction to gadgets, loves, loves, LOVES Mrs Hinch, TikTok and Candy Crush and enjoys a gin or two. She is a wonderful mum and adores our kids , doting on them day and night, much to their disgust.

She is ridiculously clever and talented, with a degree in Podiatric Medicine, fiercely loyal and great to be around.

In Black Country spayke, "her's bostin". I know I'm a very lucky man and punching way above my weight.

Now at this point I have to mention the M word. I'm not going to use all the corny gags for cheap laughs – I know my audience and I'm steering well clear of that one. Missus H is going through that period in her life right now – we've talked it over and she's explained to me that I should be prepared for mood swings, there will be emotional outbursts and a higher than usual occurrence of incoherent mumblings.

Even though I'm a grade one buffoon, as all men are, I'm not that stupid not to listen and take notice. She's my life partner and soulmate – she's a fabulous mother, wonderful wife and has stood by me through thick and thin. More than once she's saved our marriage.

I owe her everything.

In saying that, she did give me permission to write the stuff about her on the condition that I don't use the M word as a prop for rubbish jokes.

So I won't.

Let's crack on.

There are so many, sooo many, things about this Wonder Woman I don't understand. We have been together more than half our adult lives, so you'd think by now I would have grasped some sort of comprehension, some sort of insight into her way of thinking. But no, she's as mysterious to me now as she was all those years ago when we met in Brierley Hill High Street (true story – tell ya later).

I'm not alone in this fog of feminine confusion. When I occasionally speak to my fellow chubby, middle-aged husband mates (all huddled together for comfort, nursing flat pints in a dark pub, talking in in very low, hushed tones just in case any woman hears us) it's amazing how we all ~~complain~~ talk about the same things, almost to the point that we sometimes forget whose wife we're ~~complaining~~ talking about.

Here's one that's cropped up a few times - are all married women in the world all in the same WhatsApp group?

I ask because every Grumpy Middle-Aged Husband I've ever met seems to be married to the <u>same</u> woman, just in different physical form... they all say and do the same things, each one as baffling as the next, almost as if it's one big, plotted conspiracy to baffle and bemuse...

I can just imagine all the married women in the world, swapping giggly, Prosecco or gin fuelled WhatsApp messages about how they befuddled their husbands that day:

"So today I got Jeff to cut the front and back lawns by promising him "something special" tonight. He was a bit miffed when it was a one-off Alan Titchmarsh documentary about disabled dogs"

"My Derek was "on a promise" if he did the tip run. Shame I had to pop out to mum's and then went to bed early with a headache. On the plus side I've got more room in the garage now for those new puppy toys".

"I told my Jim I'd let him go up the tradesmen's entrance and smash me back doors in today. He was a bit peeved when I made him go round the back garden and knock the lean to down".

Another hot topic (!) is the heating. I can personally vouch for this based on the crazy spectrum of heating experienced in my own house.

Missus H, unsurprisingly, is in charge of the heating, which essentially means there are only two settings she's comfortable with. Everyone in the house is either freezing like an Arctic penguin or we're being slowly roasted to death, with nothing in between.

I know what to expect as soon as I get home and open the front door, which is also a good guide to Missus H's mood. As the door opens, I'm either met with a cold icy blast or a warm savannah breeze.

To be honest, it's usually the latter as she's permanently nesh, and I can tell the house is hot from some distance as I drive home – we live at the bottom of a remote hill and I can see from a half a mile away that the house has a Ready Brek glow around it and the next-door neighbour is cooking bacon and eggs on me roof tiles.

Me and the kids have got accustomed to the house slow-cooking us at a balmy 32 degrees / 89 Fahrenheit / gas mark 6 over the years and have taken to living in the house in swimwear. A bit like being in one of them false sub-tropical gardens they build at crap suburban leisure centres. Or like those netted enclosures at petting zoos where they keep big butterflies.

I swear I've come home from work some days and there's parrots nesting in the guttering. More than once we've had the police helicopter circling above with the heat seeking camera, convinced we've got a grow in the loft.

And even at this temperature, Missus H will still sit watching the telly or Crushing Candy wrapped in a comfy blanket with three sets of pyjamas on.

Oh, and there's another thing – the body heat. One minute she's having a hot flush, the next she's bitter cold.

She has more costume changes than Elton John, especially at bedtime or in the middle of the night.

Some nights her top half is cold so she slips into bed with just pants on but with a vest, sweatshirt, hoodie and a bobble hat.

Next night, it's the bottom half that's cold so she'll jump into bed wearing ski salopettes, thick socks and nipple tassles.

Oh, bedtime is fun.

Over the last few years, she has developed an entire routine designed to not only aid sleep but also ensure that every part of her body is propped or covered up. It started with ear plugs – fair enough as I know I'm a snorer.

Then there was the eye mask.

Then she had retainers in her gob.

Then she started wearing a neck support.

Then finally this contraption turned up that's supposed to aid posture – it looks a bit like a pillow in the shape of a letter H and she shoves it between her legs to make sure her pelvic floor is supported. I call it the Cock Blocker.

Add in all the extra layers of clothes she needs when she's cold and it's basically like sleeping with an ice hockey goalie.

Another grumbly topic of discussion in the pub is the car – I'm not precious about my motor like some blokes so Missus H uses it a lot.

My theory is that Missus H possesses some kind of supernatural "petrol sponge" power over my car. I swear to god - I've filled my car up, lobbed her the keys so she can "just pop out" and by the time she's back a few hours later, the needle's gone way past the big red E.

And the car seems to have taken on a strange atmosphere all its own. It's shaken, like it's met with some sort of minor disturbance. When I get in, I can hear the car let out a relieved sigh.

The heating is all to pot, with one half of the car red hot and the other freezing with the air vents pointing out the windows or napkins stuffed in em to suppress the air (Missus H confessed to doing this as the air "was drying me eyeballs up"), the radio has been totally re-tuned with only Kisstory available as a pre-select, the washer fluid is all gone and the back seat is covered in mess - phone charger leads, wine bottles, false eyelashes, items of clothing, handbags – it looks like a small hen party have ended the night there.

And the driver's seat... it's always left in a setting that even the manufacturer couldn't have dreamed up. When I get the car back, the driver's seat is either in one of two positions.

As she's only little ("I'm not little, I'm fun sized"), the first position is where the seat is tucked right underneath the steering wheel with the lumber support down and the seat back reclined - it looks like she's bob-sledded the car through the Black Country traffic, viewing the world through a periscope to weave her way home.

Then there's the second position – again, seat tucked right underneath the steering wheel, but this time with the back rest tilted right forward, steering wheel down low. I think this sitting position is so she can steer with her chin and knees, leaving her hands free to get to a new level on Candy Crush.

There are other, equally baffling instances that I don't get. For instance, there's the morning routine of starting to talk to me whilst I'm still half-asleep brushing my teeth and then getting offended when I don't answer the question I didn't hear.

Or the same when she carries on a conversation even though she's started the hair dryer and I CAN'T HEAR A WORD SHE'S SAYING.

Or when she asks me if I want anything from the shop even though she's got no money.

I love this one – "Don't tell me to be careful. It's like you don't think I know what I'm doing"

Or when she changes her mind halfway through the day about going out tonight but forgets that she didn't tell me and then has a go at me for not remembering that we weren't going out tonight ("I did tell you – you just don't listen. Keep up, monkey boy")

And what does she find to keep talking about with "the girls|" and just how looooooong is a Girlie Goodbye? Missus H will be on the drive saying goodbye for ages after a Girls Night Out. I know shoplifters who have served less time than it takes for her to say tara to her mates.

I could go on, but I won't as I quite like staying married and she might read this (doubt it).

But then it all comes back to those curves and that smell... my god it's heaven and she has **all** the curves. As soon as I, or any man in my dopey position, get an eyeful of soft, curvy flesh, a flash of a bra strap or big nose filling whiff of perfume, all previous befuddlements are quickly lost to a quick burst of testosterone-fuelled endorphins and our muddled, nookie loving brains turn to mush, ready to be morphed and moulded into whatever she wants us to do.

And I love her with all of my heart.

The next few weeks together will be the longest time we've been without the kids since they've been on the planet, so it's going to be... ermmm... interesting.

Right, I've told you about me, the kids and now Missus H. It's time to get ready to go to America!

(* as an example of my buffoonery, I've just had to go an ask her what year we met. My original guess was only four years out).

Humerica

Travel Day Part 1 - The last minute dash of the anxious housewife

Travel Day started with the realisation that we have seriously, <u>seriously</u> overestimated how much luggage we're taking.

Not long after we booked this holiday, and based on all previous baggage-laden holidays where I had been transformed into a human Buckaroo, Missus H and I sat down for a proper chat to discuss "the luggage situation". You know, one of those proper married couple chats where secretly you know you're both talking utter nonsense but you both go along with it anyway.

Basically, these chats always follow the same path and end in the same way - we talk about things until she eventually sees sense and agrees with me, then she'll go and do whatever she thinks is best. When questioned at a later date, there'll always be a moment when she was *going* to tell me she'd changed her mind or the plan, but she couldn't because at that exact, precise moment I was asleep. Or drunk. Or not in. And then she forgot. Oh, and I need to get over myself and stop acting like some sort of Victorian husband.

The main topic of the "proper luggage chat" was the amount of useless stuff we always end up taking on holiday that we never, <u>ever</u> end up needing. And because we were staying in a few different hotels while we were away, I suggested that it might be easier if we try to reduce the number of rollers and shoes she needed.

In fact, I put a very strong, and if I may add, very eloquent argument, that this time we should see if we can just survive with carry-on luggage only...

ONLY take the bare minimum needed for a few weeks in the sun - bikinis, floppy hats, sarongs... you know, the absolute essentials (not sure what Missus H was taking).

It turns out that by the time we'd packed up, we had more baggage than Katie Price and it looked like we were about to emigrate to Disney and start a new life in the British bit of Epcot.

Our combined luggage was 96 kilos.

Yes, NINETY SIX KILOS.

And I've only got one t shirt that fits me and hides me moobs and one pair of elasticated waist shorts. What else are we taking? (It was at this point I seriously had to ask her if she'd smuggled the dog in. She hadn't, but I did find a squeaky toy she'd bought to remind her of Molly).

The build up to this travel day had been manic. Making sure Molly the Cockapoo had enough kibble, paying the window cleaner his January invoice and trying to shoe horn 1 litre of Vosene shampoo in to 10 x 100 ml bottles (like it makes a difference). And as we were leaving the kids "Home Alone" for three weeks, we had to write down instructions for almost every single domestic appliance. Including the toaster.

And we had rows. We had rows about which is the right plug adapter, how many pairs of identical strappy sandals she needed (all of them, apparently) and whether it was ok for a chubby middle-aged man to wear a fanny pack.

Now, I do like a fanny pack. Not only because it makes me giggle like a schoolboy but also because it's a convenient way to carry all my stuff without hurting my shoulders. And because it also hides my belly (I am the shape of Winnie The Pooh after a days binge on the hunny)

AND, amazingly, I went to school with a girl called Fanny Pack.

Honest.

We became great friends at school and we did domestic science together. She was ace at baking, long before that wrinkled prune Mary Berry made it trendy, and her speciality was muffins - they were amazing! I tried really hard to copy her but, try as I might, my muffins never tasted as nice as Fanny's.

In the end Missus H, relented on the condition

that if I'm taking a fanny pack, she could squeeze in yet another identical pair of beige wedges.

It was very nearly time to leave the Black Country and head to Heathrow, but before we nearly bost the car's suspension, and added the extra trailer for the luggage, Missus H had to do her usual trick of checking round the house from top to bottom so it's nice and tidy if we get burgled.

While she's doing this, I sulk moodily round the house looking at my watch as it gets progressively further away from the time we'd agreed to leave, periodically shouting up the stairs: "Can we go now please?"

It amazes me how she finds things that all of a sudden are <u>dead</u> urgent and need her undivided attention <u>now</u>, just at the precise moment we're heading away for a pre-planned three weeks.

Eventually, after she'd cleaned the fridge, fed the dog, wiped down the skirting boards, fixed the loft hatch, mended the broken tap, turned up the hem on her skirt, called her mate to say "It's Our Turn!", paid the council tax and fed the dog again cos she'd got hungry in the meantime, we jumped into the car and left Grumpy Towers headed for Heathrow airport where we have a night booked in a convenient but terribly expensive airport hotel.

On the way down, Missus H passed the time

simultaneously playing Candy Crush (she's a black belt), Snapchatting me whilst driving so I looked like a chauffeuring puppy dog and flicking through her weather app to see what the weather's like where we're going.

And 15 places where we've been in the last ten years.

"Oooh, look! It's 32 and sunny in Orlando...

18 and misty in Magaluf...

it's only 16 and cloudy in Skibbereen..."

I have no idea why she does this. What difference does it make? It's pointless!

It's like when people say "Oooh, this time last week we were in Applebees..." or "Three weeks' time we'll be in Walmart buying Caramel M & M's..." So what? You're here NOW, you can't be in two places at once.

You know that saying, if my aunty had a dick he'd be my uncle?

Yeah? That's what I mean.

By the way, that phrase was invented by my Aunty Derek.

We checked in quite late at the hotel so took full advantage of the fact that no-one was around and nicked two luggage trollies to stash our EIGHT bags and settled in for a 5 hour sleep, which at the hotel room rate works out at £40 an hour.

At some point in my nightly ablutions, I realised that despite having combined luggage that would be more than Bear Grills needs to conquer Everest, I had no toothpaste. Worse still, in an attempt to "save weight" Missus H had bought a "Travel" toothbrush and toothpaste that was absolutely miniscule. It looked like it had come straight out of Sylvanian Doll's House accessories section and was no use to her at all.

Missus H has great teeth, but they are on the large side for her cute little mouth – we once got stopped at airport security cos they thought she was smuggling ivory.

So, with bad breath and a rising sense of anxiety about the long flight tomorrow, we nodded off for some restless sleep.

I've got loads more to tell you about Travel Day, so join me again in the next chapter for the bit that I hate – the flight.

Travel Day Part 2 – Beating the fear of flying via mind power (and vodka)

I awoke with a start, as I often do when in a strange hotel room and tried to cling on to the remnants of a weird dream about Fanny Pack, my old schoolmate and the inspiration for a joke in the previous chapter.

Cruel thing about dreams – they disappear like a puff of smoke the second you wake up, but you're always left with that little teaser about something interesting, or something that was just about to happen. Unless you're a married woman – in which case you seem to wake up every morning in a permanent and unprovoked bad mood as you've just had a dream that your husband has eloped with your best mate.

Anyway, picking up from where we left off, Missus H and I were in an airport hotel, just about to head off to Heathrow Terminal 3 to catch our flight to America.

I'd been dead busy with work in the build up to this holiday, so I'd let her have a go at researching and booking the flights this time, which I think she quite enjoyed. Hence, some time back she excitedly shouted from the front room and asked me to quickly choose between a Norwegian and a Virgin - for a giddy moment I thought she was watching Babestation.

I plumped for Virgin for me air miles, although Norwegian was a lot cheaper if you didn't mind being in a seat with less leg room than Rip Ride Rockit, crop spraying and travelling via Greenland.

Bags loaded into the motor, we were off to the meet and greet bang on the appointed time. We met a lovely chap of indeterminable descent and questionable accent and handed him the keys to our new £30,000.00 Audi so he could go and park it in a farmer's field in Essex. Well, he seemed like a nice chap and he had got a clipboard AND a Hi-Viz jacket, so it's all kosher, right?

Safely checked in with the tightly clothed Virgin Check-in Girls (is it me or do they make their uniforms deliberately small, to emphasise the curves?), it was on to security and the ritual humiliation of the full body scan and doing the "Try to get your belt back on before your jeans drop down whilst standing on one foot dance".

Why, why, WHY is the only person that has never flown / stupidest person in aviation history ALWAYS in front of me in the security queue?

This always happens to me - I'm a worldly-wise traveller so I know the drill. Coat off, laptop out, freezer bag with nail polish remover in the tray, all metal objects in your bag (except for the "personal" piercings which I have to quietly whisper about into his / her ear, obviously.

They're a bugger to get out and worse to get back in) and after the "stick em up" dab in the big microwave so the perv behind the screen can see my JD Sports pants, I'm proven to be no threat to airline security and fit to fly.

But, no matter where I'm flying from or going to, I always have in front of me some shuffling, bumbling idiot who, just at the rushed moment when it all needs to happen, suddenly realises that they have left a family sized bottle of Fanta, an entire set of steak knives and a litre of fabric conditioner in their carry on.

The bloke in front of me today had bought his collection of flick-knives that he thought was ok cos they were in a SEE-THROUGH PLASTIC BAG...!!

How on earth do people not know what to do when they get to the security check? I mean, there's umpteen signs, it's on your boarding pass and there is literally a member of staff walking up and down the sweaty queue, telling people what they need to do next.

This is the same type of person that queues for ages at a till, then when it comes to pay let out a shriek of surprise as if they didn't know shopping costs actual money and spends the next 5 minutes ferreting around in a Mary Poppins type handbag trying to find their purse, and then pay in counted out 2 pence pieces cos all their coupons have expired.

Rant over.

Safely through security, we made our way down the snaking, labyrinthian corridor of perfume, designer sunglasses and giant Toblerones , managing to avoid the old hags who want to spray you with smelly chemicals and camp blokes who offer you a thimble full of Japanese Scotch Whiskey.

Then on to my least favourite shop in the world – WH Smith. I have to go to Smiths as it's the only place I can get big bottles of apple juice that act as the carrier for my smuggled vodka, but Jesus Christ Almighty do I fucking hate that shop. I covered this in the last book, so I won't repeat myself here. Suffice to say that the fuckwit who decided to sack all the till staff and replace them with patronising, robotic scanners that break down every five minutes needs to have his / her intestines gouged out with a plastic spoon whilst still alive and his / her genitalia continually walloped with a table tennis bat. That is all.

After Smiths, it's on to another favourite, Boots cos the water is a quid cheaper and it gives me a chance to work out what exactly is in the Boots Meal Deal.

Note to airport Boots (and other chemists / supermarkets / newsagents) – don't you think it would be a good idea to put the stuff that's included IN the Meal Deal, clearly marked and

ACTUALLY CLOSE <u>TO</u> THE FUCKING Meal Deal?

This would save us all so much time and prevent many items being abandoned at the till when you realise that the Egg and Cress Sandwich Meal Deal does not actually include a litre of Lucozade and a tub of KY Jelly. It would also prevent travelling numpties (the same numpties who don't know how to get through security) constantly asking your staff "Is this in the Meal Deal, love?" whilst holding up a ham and cheese baguette, a copy of The Sun and a bumper pack of Veet wax strips.

Provisions sorted, it's off to the pre-booked convenient but terribly expensive lounge where I always attempt to drink my own body weight in vodka and nick as many mini muffins as I can squeeze into my rucksack. And fruit, teabags, sugar, cutlery... nothing is safe (my all-time record is a gallon of apple juice).

I'm not a fan of flying. My brain can't comprehend how such a massive structure, packed with people, fuel, food and my 96 kilos of luggage can get out of first gear, never mind jump up into the air. In order to help my brain comprehend, I have to bend it a little with a Michael Hadley Cocktail, the recipe of which I won't pass on here for fear of being banned by the CAA. Suffice to say, by the time I get on the plane, I'm a much more relaxed, happier, dopier version of myself and wouldn't mind at all if the cabin crew asked me to sit outside.

And so after an hour or so of hard booze in the convenient but terribly expensive lounge, trying real hard to convince myself I'm really getting on a train and <u>not</u> about to spend 11 hours trapped in a metal Smarties tube with filing cabinet grade metal wings filled with highly combustible fuel, the departure board changed to "Boarding", Missus H wiped the dribble from my chin and frog marched me like a misbehaving toddler to the boarding gate, where she gently pushed me on to the plane.

The clever guy trusted with flying us all over to the US in this hunk of expensive shiny metal was, surprisingly, an American by the name of Captain Tucker-Bob Billy-Ray Hunter Junior the third.

It wasn't a surprise that he was American, it was just a surprise he wasn't shouting.

(Apologies to any male American readers, but why don't you have a volume control like the rest of the world? Why do you need to be so constantly loud? Life isn't a bawdy shouting competition you know... Have you never heard of a whisper?)

As we settled in, I couldn't help let out a whoop of joy and a secret fist pump when I spotted that the seat behind me was occupied by a young kid with young (little) legs, meaning that I'd be able to recline without fear of being tutted at. Unfortunately, my joy was short lived as halfway through the flight he was substituted for his dad who was evidently a body double for Giant Haystacks.

To help ease my nerves and kill time on the flight, I always smuggle a selection of booze and sometimes snacks with me. I also knew that as we're flying Premium Economy (shorthand for "I've maxed out the credit card but still not as rich as people in Upper Class") we'd be fed with copious amounts of salty, fatty, chocolatey snacks at any point we needed them.

Which, in my case, this was going to be A LOT,

So in preparation I asked for an extension seat belt - not that I needed one but cos I'm planning on getting my money's worth by nibbling Beardy Bransons Lunchbox.

That's not a euphemism, by the way.

(Although if it gets me extra air miles, give us a tinkle Dicky Boy. Bet you've got one of them red uniforms to fit me, you old stud muffin xxxx...)

Three hours into the flight, I'd consumed so much my cankles had ballooned and I looked like a blowfish. Unable to focus on the film in front of me, Toy Story 4 which I'd somehow managed to play in Japanese with Chinese subtitles, I drifted into a gin and Frazzles induced coma.

Which Missus H was dead happy about as it meant she could partake in one of her favourite pastimes - inspecting my weathered face whilst I'm asleep. She does this A LOT. I'll frequently wake up to her hovering menacingly over me with one big inquisitive eye, looking for a juicy blackhead to squeeze or some rich scrapings of ear wax. Her current favourite is nostril hair gardening – she checks the length while I'm having a power nap and when they're just right, uses the extra sharp tweezers to yank em out just as I'm about to wake up.

I was spared the humiliation this time as we were in a crowded cabin, which was lucky for me as my nostril hair had grown an inch or two since we took off and I could sense her getting dizzy with excitement.

The rest of the flight passed in a haze. This is all I can remember:

I ate. I drank. I slept. Woke up.

I ate. I drank. I slept. Woke up.

I ate. I drank. I slept. Woke up.

We landed. In America.

Obviously, we landed otherwise I wouldn't be writing this would I?

We were bound to spend the next few days in LA, then a working road trip through California with a little bit of sightseeing on the way, before heading off to our real holiday to Orlando.

PS – Missus H wanted to let you all know it was 13 and foggy in Skibbereen.

Welcome to California!

Sponsored by Vibes CBD oil

When we eventually got through US Immigration, collected all of our many, many bags and dodged the suspicious looking cop sitting on the "Nothing to Declare" stool, we were released into arrivals in the inner sanctum of Los Angeles airport and joined the throngs at what appeared to be coffee break at the Annual California Stoners Convention.

Man, I knew Californians were laid back, but I never expected this. There were junkies everywhere - some of them giggling, some slumped up a corner in a dopey haze and others babbling away in some weird language like some demented preacher.

And that was just the air crew.

Astonished, we pushed on through the spaced-out crowd, refusing little whispered offers of "sniff" as we went, trying to work out where to meet our pre-booked taxi. One weird looking guy kept shuffling up to me and saying "dope" which I thought was very rude.

Outside, it was even worse – I couldn't work out if we'd stumbled into a live film set for The Walking Dead or if LAX was the setting for a genuine zombie outbreak.

In fact, for a brief moment, and bearing in mind I was still under the influence of a wild cocktail of booze, horse tranquilizers and sugary snacks myself, I panicked at the thought that maybe I'd dreamt the whole flight and just woke up in West Bromwich.

Most of them were so smacked off their tits they were no harm to anyone but themselves and the imaginary friend they all seemed to be talking to. And they were all rather jolly. Not surprising really as there was a very evident and heady pong of skunk in the air, and the longer we waited the more I could feel myself relax.

By the time our taxi driver, Dexter Riddley, turned up, Missus H was giggling like a little schoolgirl and I was seriously considering swapping all my jeans for harem pants. I also desperately wanted a kebab.

We snapped back into reality and stumbled into the back of the cab, where we proceeded to spend the next one and a half hours travelling just 5 miles in the legendary Los Angeles traffic.

My first impression of LA was not that great to be honest – I was only mildly kidding about the stoners (it got progressively worse the longer we stayed, especially in some of the "downtown" areas) and the panorama on the journey from the airport to our digs was no different to being stuck trying to get back to the Black Country via Spaghetti Junction.

Anyhoo, after a lurching ride along the freeways of LA battling against sleep, we eventually arrived at our base for the next three nights. We had chosen to stay in Long Beach for no other reason than I sort of expected to be on a beach and the hotels were a bit cheaper than the ones close to downtown LA.

It turns out that not only were we not on a beach, but I really should have checked the maps on Booking.com. The hotel itself was nice enough, especially if you're a fan of ocean transport, shipping containers and 24-hour naval activity outside your bedroom window. (I've since found out that Long Beach Container Port is one of the world's busiest seaports, and a leading gateway for trade between the United States and Asia. It supports more than 2.6 million jobs nationally and generates billions of dollars in economic activity throughout the US. It also handles more than 7.5 million 20-foot container units (TEUs) each year. It also has a great Wikipedia page).

But the view was fine if you looked the other way and tried to drown out the foghorns and the rooms were nice, so once we were checked in we dumped our cases, holdalls, backpacks and duty free and fell exhausted into bed.

*****

Jet lag is lovely isn't it?

One minute you're absolutely zonked out, fast asleep having a lovely dream (in my case, usually about Holly Willoughby or Nigella Lawson) and then the next you're wide awake - wired, buzzing and filled with adrenaline. And no matter how hard you crave for more sleep, your brain just won't slow down and tap, tap, taps away until eventually you give up and go on Facebook.

Even if you do try to beat it and lie curled up, ready for sleep with controlled breathing and all your best relaxation techniques, your brain still finds a way to plant some outlandish thought in your head that absolutely guarantees you're not nodding off any time soon.

In the middle of the night, I was trying to stop myself from thinking about how I could persuade Barry Manilow to get in touch with my mum to wish her a happy 70th birthday. Or how it would be a great idea to tarmac our front garden over just cos I'd broken the mower a few days before we left.

Eventually, I ended up compiling a list of things I would ban from American hotel rooms if I were ever elected President (and let's face it, even I could do a better job than Donald Spunk Trumpet). Here we go:

1) Low baths that think they're oblong showers
2) Very low toilets with a very high-water table

3) American coffee machines

There are many other things I could have also included on that list. I stay in a lot of hotels and have found lots to moan about. For example, and this isn't exclusive to American hotels by any means, the pathetic, pitiful little bins that are lined with a wrinkled, gossamer thin excuse of a bin liner that acts like an airbag as soon as you throw in a sweet wrapper. Or the alternative but equally useless miniature pedal bin that actively tries to _run away_ the second that you step on it.

Top of the list of things I'd change is that bath / shower thing.

Is it a low bath or a big shower? Or a Belfast sink on steroids?

It's the rest room equivalent of a confused transgender teen - not deep enough to be a bath but totally the wrong design to be a big shower. If it's supposed to be a bath it's a total flop as the water barely covers your chubby bits, and it's too small and the wrong shape to be a shower. The shower curtain, which is always cold, somehow finds a way to wrap itself around you like clingfilm on a hot sausage and the shower head is either too far away, trapped at the wrong angle or dribbles a weak stream of liquid like your grandad after two pints of stout.

Next on the list is the ridiculously low toilet. Which would be ok if it weren't for the ridiculously high water level. This annoying combination brings a whole new dimension to a man's visit to the loo, especially mine. Not to go into too much detail, but I do like a "sit", regardless of the reason to "go" – yet another thing that happens to hunky men like me as they get older.

(No-one warns you about this – the slow, tortuous slide into old age and the depressing arrival of night-time loo trips. At my age, I know that at some point in the night I'll definitely need a wee, and most of the time I even manage to make it to the bathroom).

This plays out every night in our house – I'm probably having a dream about Holly Willoughby or Nigella Lawson which gets interrupted by an increasingly loud alarm bell in my head telling me that the dam defences are about to be breached. I then have to make it in time to the bathroom, feeling my way in a blind stagger with arms outstretched like some sort of shuffling, chubby mummy, all the time not trying to trip over the dog. Then, post piddle, I have to make it back into my warm bed before my brain realises that I'm awake and proceeds to keep me up all night. God, I hate getting old).

Back home on my own Black Country loo this isn't a problem and I can spend ages happily tatting on my phone whilst waiting for the bomb doors to open, or having a Squirty Tinkle -

which, funnily enough, was my drag queen name at school.

But here in the States, the toilet design means that there is barely a fag paper between your undercarriage and recycled bog water, meaning that every visit to the loo is like a game of Russian Bell End Roulette. I find myself hovering above the seat, to afraid that if I sit down my willy is gonna be plunged into icy cold water and end up shrinking back up. And you don't need that at my age, trust me.

I've saved my biggest grumble til last – the American hotel coffee machine. I've moaned about this in my other books but obviously no-one from the US hospitality industry was reading.

What fuckwit thought this was a good idea, having a microwave sized contraption with no discernible method of use that can only produce half a cup full of tepid coffee after 5 minutes' worth of brewing?

I hate these things with a passion. They invariably come with an ozone layer bosting coffee making kit made of non-recyclable, live-forever, seal strangling plastic and instructions printed so small that you need a magnifying glass to make any sense of it.

Have Americans not heard of kettles?

The one in the Long Beach hotel was the worst one I've ever come across. The instructions were in size 8 font, so I took a picture of them on my phone and zoomed in to get a better look. You have to follow a set pattern to release the snappy water tank lid, pour in a paper cup's worth of tap water, firmly press the tank lid back down without severing a finger end, which then releases the magical coffee pod holder. Once you've placed your Smooth Colombian or Dirty Costa Rican pod into the holder, you then have to work out which one of the three buttons with no markings makes coffee. Good luck with that.

By process of elimination, and after much swearing and bashing of tables, AND using up all but one of the three pods generously provided at this $250 a night hotel, the following morning after a few hours of jet lagged sleep I eventually did make Missus H a "sort of" coffee. This was served in a wafer thin paper cup, tasted as bitter as my writing and contained so much caffeine that 30 minutes later she had eyes bigger than a bush baby and I had to stop her from using my toothbrush to clean the tile grout in the hotel bathroom.

Which was not that surprising as I'd told her we were going out in 5 minutes.

And out we were heading – we were off to see California.

P.S. Drizzly in Skibbereen

Travels through California

Sponsored by Radio BootScoot

Ahead of our Magical day at Disneyland California, we had the reality for the next week or so in the form of work. Well, I've got to pay for all these trips somehow...

I won't go into the boring details, but my real job (cos, believe it or not, this writing lark ay me _real_ job...) is selling parts for classic cars and conveniently there just so happens to be thousands of them over in California. In fact, hundreds of thousands of em, so I reckon that if I can bag a few new customers while I'm over here it would give me an excuse to keep coming back.

If only there was a classic car garage in Cars Land I'd be sorted...

To be truthful, it would probably help my career no end if I knew something about classic cars, which I don't - the only thing that I do know about them cars is that there's a nut behind the steering wheel.

I have the greatest job in the world, travelling to some amazing, exciting places and get to see some of the world's most incredible (and expensive) cars. But it's totally wasted on me – a bit like working in the porn industry and not liking boobs.

This week's work came in the form of a very long, hot road trip from Los Angeles up to San Francisco, with several stop offs in between to try to impress potential American customers with my Black Country accent and distinct lack of knowledge. I know you haven't bought this book to learn about the difficulties in trying to create a 6 volt charging system for the 1954 Porsche 356, so instead here are a couple of my observations about life on the West Coast of America, as seen through the eyes of a weary traveller.

First of all, the people are really friendly and love Brits. We met some amazing folks along the way and every single one was polite, courteous and hospitable. It's very refreshing to meet people who are not only well mannered but genuinely pleased to meet you. I guess that was like Britain before we got all moody.

Most parts of the west coast are breathtakingly beautiful, from soaring mountains to gorgeous beaches. Santa Barbara was a favourite of ours, followed closely by Santa Monica and the iconic pier. San Francisco was miles better than LA – it has a great feel about it and we had a great few nights there.

I'm going to write this next bit in my serious voice.

** adopts dulcet, earthy tone of Sir Trevor McDonald or similar **

Two things that are evident in California is the sorry plight of the homeless and the massive problem with drugs, both of which are utterly heart-breaking. Especially when you witness that "normal" Californians are so used to it that they see right through the poor souls as though they were invisible. We experienced this many times over a week of travelling, and it never stopped shocking us. These people slumped in doorways or shuffling around the streets in an opioid cloud are normal human beings, with brothers, sisters, families. It could be someone's precious son – someone's cherished daughter. They had a life before where someone would have loved them yet here they are all alone, left to see out their days trapped in hellish torment and in plain sight of the rest of their fellow Americans.

What have we come to as a society if we can so easily overlook the plight of fellow human beings and treat them as nothing more than skin and bone?

None of this is helped by the fact that healthcare in America is not free to all, resulting in compounding levels of ill health which in turn perpetuates the problem as the population grows and becomes more unhealthy, more obese, and increasingly addicted to drugs and alcohol. The homeless and drug addicts are far less likely to afford healthcare, so they further descend into the depths of society until there is literally nowhere to go and no help available.

Doesn't it make you realise how lucky we are to have the NHS?

I've witnessed homelessness before and I understand that we are not without our own drug problems in the UK, but I have never seen anything like that before. It's a national tragedy – and likely to get much worse.

*****

Moving the mood dial up a notch and swiftly back to my camp Noddy Holder voice, here's another thing that happens to you when you get older and the flab turns up - your taste in music tends to broaden and become much more varied. As the years pass and you mellow and become a more rounded person, you get a newfound interest in different music and a greater admiration and understanding of artists that you previously thought were wank.

For instance, a while back I developed an appreciation of classical music – I found that it helped me to relax and for a few sweet moments in my hectic day, it drowned out the incessant screaming in my head. I loved the way it could instantly transport me into a different world, one where I felt more relaxed and at peace with myself and my surroundings. I couldn't get enough - the soft strings, the booming drums and spectacular symbol crashes.

I can't claim to be an expert by any stretch of the imagination and I'd listen to anything on Classic FM, but I did especially like the work of Mozart, Jean-Paul Gaultier and Van Gogh.

More recently though, I've found myself tuning away from my usual diet of Elbow, The Jam and Barry Manilow in favour of a totally different genre - Country and Western.

I reckon I've always had a liking for Country and Western music, but it's not until now I fully "got" it, if you know what I mean. Somewhere deep in the recesses of my brain, I think I gained an affection for it from my early years - I'd like to think it's from being around my grandad Walter as a child, listening to him sing good 'ole country tunes and watching grainy, black and white cowboy films starring John Wayne and Robert Mitchum. These butch, manly men became my heroes and all through my childhood I told everyone I was gonna be John Wayne when I grew up.

Which would have been a waste of time as there's not much call for cowboys in Dudley.

But in all honesty, I think it was Dolly Parton that aroused my interest. I can't quite put my finger on it but there's a couple of things about Dolly that made this teenage Black Country boy get a little giddy and experience a very specific rush of blood.

I get my daily fix of Country and Western from a UK radio station called, rather imaginatively, Country Tracks Radio, which originally started out as a women's hospital radio. I think it's been put together on a budget as they don't seem able to afford many songs – if you were to listen for two hours, I reckon you'd hear the same song played three separate times.

One of which I'm going to share with you now as it's stuck in my head and I think it deserves to be stuck in yours too. It's a beautiful love song by an American guy by the name of Brad Paisley called "I'm Still a Guy".

At this point, I need a little audience participation, something you don't usually get from a book. Don't forget I'm in your head now, never to leave...

Please do this for me – shout "**ALEXA!** Play I'm Still A guy by Brad Paisley!" Or YouTube it. Either way, I'm not fussed as long as you do.

Now, please.

Hurry up, I've got a chapter to tell.

Brad sings about a subject that has affected all of us hunky stud muffins at some point in our lives – namely how he's managed to hang on to his rugged manliness in the face of rising, Poncey metrosexuality.

Oooh, I know that battle Brad, and I feel your pain love, I honestly do... Shut that door...

In the song, he captures the very essence of still being a tough, butch caveman who wants to drink beer, pick fights and shag like a rabbit, despite the rest of the world around him growing up and moving on.

Here's a few of my favourite lyrics:

*"**When you see a deer you see Bambi
And I see antlers up on the wall
When you see a lake you think picnic
And I see a large mouth up under that
log**"*

I think what Brad means by "a large mouth up under that log" is a particularly big fish which he would like to catch instead of sitting on a blanket eating a scotch egg. Or it could mean blow job (I don't know – I don't speak American).

*"**When you see a priceless French
painting
I see drunk, naked girls
You think that riding a wild bull sounds
crazy
And I'd like to give it a whirl**"*

From this, I reckon that Brad never really got the Renaissance Period of the 14th century and wasn't a fan of Botticelli or Fernando Botero like some of his more educated country girlfriends. Shame really as the lighting and shade on *The*

Birth of Venus is quite something and the way Botticelli brought the subject to life in a solely sensory aspect still amazes art lovers to this day. And she had great tits.

"I'll pour out my heart
Hold your hand in the car
Write a love song that makes you cry
Then turn right around knock some jerk
to the ground
'Cause he copped a feel as you walked by"

Now isn't that a beautiful verse? I think it sums up the dynamic between a loving, caring woman and an imbecilic, low brow thug with a short fuse and a tendency for violence.

"These days there's dudes getting facials
Manicured, waxed and botoxed
With deep spray-on tans and creamy
lotiony hands
You can't grip a tackle-box

With all of these men lining up to get
neutered
It's hip now to be feminized
I don't highlight my hair
I've still got a pair
Yeah honey, I'm still a guy"

And who wouldn't want a man like Brad? With his cracked skin, grey hair and fingernails covered in grease, oil and snot. He's a keeper, girls.

And then the big tear-jerking last verse...

*"All my eyebrows ain't plucked
There's a gun in my truck
Oh thank God, I'm still a guy"*

When he says "All my eyebrows" I assume just the two main ones. Although by the sounds of the lyrics it does appear that despite an amazing singing voice and an obvious talent for writing, Brad is evolving at a much slower speed and on a different planet to the rest of us, so maybe he has got a third (or fourth) eye. And maybe very hard skin on the back of his hand where his knuckles still drag along.

Anyway, I hope you've enjoyed that and now I've "shown you the light" in musical terms, maybe you'll listen to all of the 11 songs they have on Country Tracks Radio.

Let's get back to the story.

So, here I am – a chubby middle-aged man from the Black Country with a love for America culture, motoring through the wide open roads of California with my best gal, listening to proper, authentic Country and Western music being pumped into my ears by the DJ's of such fine radio stations as Cowboy FM, Redneck Radio and Rootin Tootin Rock.

We rocked from LA to Pasadena, from Santa Monica to Monterey and all the time we never moved the dial on the radio. It was country heaven.

There is nothing better to lift your mood than a sad song about yer wife running off with yer sister or yer dog being thrashed to puppy chunks by a combine harvester set to a fast double bass beat with a backdrop of thrashing banjos.

Bloody great.

The music (and news, weather and traffic) is regularly interrupted by adverts that have obviously been carefully matched to the demographic profile of the listeners. So, it's quite normal to hear cleverly thought out plugs with catchy jingles, say for example, the local machine gun shop, equipment for making moonshine or repairing tractors.

Or massive discounts off new Ku Klux Klan whites.

In between the adverts, they occasionally play some songs and on one long trip along the Californian freeway it was our pleasure to be tuned into DJ Hogan Ridley III, who was selecting some real barnfloor fillers.

As we headed toward Santa Monica in the late afternoon sunshine, I turned up the volume and for the next few hours we were treated to such Country and Western classics as "*Get yer tongue outta my mouth cos I'm kissing you goodbye*" by Troy Deeney, then a few belters from Conway

Twitty including "*I still miss you baby, but my aims getting better*" followed by "*I'm so miserable without you it's like having you here*".

Just before the adverts about discount cattle feed at Ol' McDonalds Farm and the weekends book burning, Hogan switched it up a notch with the all-time great from Jaxon Johnny Jackson, "*I hate every bone in your body except mine*".

We stopped off at a Wendys as I needed 5,000 calories and the music had put me in the mood for some Southern Country Fayre. Hunger sated by the combo meal of deep fried chicken and waffles, grits, ribs, cornbread, Tater Tots and jello, all washed down with a gallon of sweet iced tea, (Missus H had salad) I burped my way back to the car with my cowgal and we re-joined the freeway. In perfect time too as it was the start of the Lonesome Hour with DJ John-Boy Jimmy-Bob Davis Love Junior the Third.

John-Boy pulled out all the stops and knew exactly what to play to tug on those old heart strings. He had me and Missus H bawling like a West Bromwich teenager who's just been caught cheating her benefits, playing his all-time top 5 love songs... tunes that would melt any gals heart.

5 - "*You're the reason our kids are so ugly*" by Dwayne Buffet and the Turnip Pickers

4 – "*How Can I Miss You If You Won't Go*

Away" by Jethro Burns

3 – "*You Done Tore Out My Heart and Stomped That Sucker Flat*" by Blackberry Smoke

2 – "*Save A Horse, Ride A Cowboy*" – by Hank Marvin and the Bug Stompers

And staying at the number 1 spot...

1 – "*I Don't Know Whether To Kill Myself or Go Bowling*" by Sawgrass Sam and the Corndogs

We were sad to reach our destination as the God Fearin' Hour had just started. The show kicked off with the all-time classic "They Ain't Makin' Jews Like Jesus Anymore" by Skunk Diggety Dawg, and as we pulled the car into the hotel car park "Drop Kick Me Jesus, Through the Goalposts of Life" by Jonny Gullible and The Kentucky Disciples.

Top stuff.

Carry on reading – we're off to Disney next.

Twas the night before Disney...

Sponsored by The Big Butt Hinge Company Inc.

My god California hotels are expensive.

That's an understatement - they are *ridiculously* expensive... and you don't get much for your Black Country pound either.

The choices seem to be that if you want one night in a really nice hotel you will pay the same amount of money that you did for your wedding reception, or, if you "downgrade", for the equivalent price of a 4 star in the UK you will end up kipping in a "Bates" style motel where you're guaranteed to be bitten all over by bedbugs or murdered.

Or both.

So, imagine how much it is for a two-night stay in a Mr Disney property in California... it is Supercalifragilisticexpialidocious expensive. I'm no Scrooge McDuck and we're only here for 2 nights so I jumped on to a few price comparison websites and plumped for what's known as a "Disney Neighbour" hotel just a few hot shuffles away from the park entrance.

Can't recall the exact name but it was something catchy along the lines of "Anaheim Not Quite Disney Quality Inn"

Based on previous American hotel experience, and the price compared to the real Disney hotels in the same post code, we weren't expecting much so we weren't disappointed when we didn't get much.

It was a mix of hotel, conference centre and old people's home.

The kind of soulless place where fat, boorish American blokes in beige chinos and polo shirts called Chip talk loudly to each other at the annual trade exhibition of the US Door Hinge Manufacturers Association and it had all the charm of a West Bromwich clap clinic with 1980's décor.

They had tried to "Disneyfy" reception with a few out of date wonky pull up banners advertising the release of "Honey I shrunk The Kids" and "Herbie Goes Bananas" and there was a kids play area where little uns could colour in pictures of Gummi Bears or Michael Jackson. The teenagers with 25 cents could play Frogger or Pac-Man.

It could have been a whole lot worse...

On our road trip to get here, we stayed in one dodgy motel in Pasadena where the manager checking us in asked us to leave a light on at night so the rats didn't bump into the cockroaches. When we got to the room, we were surprised to find a body shaped chalk outline on the floor and all the pictures on the wall were deliberately on the skunt to cover up bullet holes.

Unperturbed, and because I'd pre-paid the room, I convinced Missus H it'd be ok, and, after I'd cleaned the blood and pubes out, persuaded her to have a nice shallow bath. I called down to reception to ask if I could get a bathroom towel and the manager said I could have one after the guy next door had finished with it.

We ended up sleeping with all our clothes on with our credit cards, passport and cash in our pants.

All for just $250.00 a night.

The "Best Western Budget Disney Neighbour Nobody Inn and Sanitorium" was luxury in comparison and the biggest threat wasn't murder but getting trapped in the lift with Billy-Bob Ray Linton Jr the Third as he explained the intricacies of the new ACME spring-loaded butt hinge.

It was too late for anything other than get ready for a big day tomorrow, so we cozied up in our room wearing Disney jamas, rented Smoky and the Bandit on VHS and scoffed Cheetos washed down with root beer before falling into a carb crash sleep.

*****

Before we get into the juicy bits, here's some fun facts about Disneyland, California:

- ➤ It is the ORIGINAL Disney theme park, despite common belief that Orlando was first.
- ➤ The plants in Tomorrowland are all edible. *
- ➤ There is a pet cemetery behind The Haunted Mansion.
- ➤ Walt Disney had his own private apartment above the fire station and his mummified remains are kept in a kitchen closet. **
- ➤ It cost me $450.00 for two one day "park hopper" tickets so I could cram in as much enjoyment as possible into 12 hours and come up with enough material for two chapters.

This is our first ever visit to the original Disneyland and to use a phrase borrowed from my new friend Denver Maverick, CEO of Analtech Hinge Co, Nebraska, who I met over a bowl of Lucky Charms at breakfast, we're both "stoked" for the day.

This is not just for the opportunity to compare the California version to the one we're more familiar with in Orlando but also because I can chalk off another thing on my bucket list - as of today I will have personally visited 5 of the Worlds' iconic theme parks:

Euro Disney in 1993
Walt Disney World Orlando (lots of times)
Shanghai Disney in 2018 & 2019
Disneyland California (today)
Black Country Museum (Annual Pass Holder)

Walt's original psycho park, Disneyland California was opened in July 1955. The park had been inspired by a fever dream after 5 days on the crackpipe, and only took one year to build. It opened with just 18 attractions, 14 of which are still there to this day, including Peter Pans Flight, Guardians of the Galaxy – Mission: Breakout, Buzz Lightyears Spinning Tops and Star Tours ***

Disneyland itself is divided into two equally hot, expensive parks – the original one called **Disneyland Park** and the newest one, opened in 2001 called, rather imaginatively, **Disney California Adventure Park**. I did wonder how long it took old Walt to come up with that name... til I realised he died in 1966 so it was probably some corporate bullshit decision after spunking $1 million on focus groups.

The original park was built on a mosquito infested swamp by Walt himself – he was a builder by trade and wanted a recreation of other, smaller fairs he'd been to with his kids back in the 1930's and 40's but with bigger rides such as ferris wheels, steamboats and carousels in a larger, hotter setting without the fear of malaria and better access to recreational drugs.

All I can say is I'm glad he never came to work on building sites back home in the Black Country and ended up in our funfairs for inspiration. I remember the first time me and my mates went to Gandeys Funfair and Circus as kids in Dudley – I was all excited to go on the rides, laugh at the clowns and see the amazing acrobats.

By the time I was picked back up by my mum, I'd been traumatised for life. I'd seen two muggings, three stabbings and someone headbutting a dog.

I'd also had my candy floss nicked and witnessed two drunken clowns having a fight behind the Bearded Lady. (She wasn't an attraction; she was just out for the night from West Bromwich).

As I got older, I realised that the "Funfair" was anything but, and the triannual visit from the Gandey family was more of a tortuous ordeal for the local community and an excuse for them to steal scrap metal, rob small businesses and pretend to tarmac people's drives.

So, yes, I'm very glad Walt never had the chance to see this for himself otherwise in the middle of Disneyland there would have been an expensive, lethal and very violent bumper cars ride manned by pikies with greased back hair, tattoos and leather vests who jump on the back of each vehicle, hanging on to the electric coat hanger thing, looking to either rob the driver in mid bump or to choose which young, underage girl he was going to bribe with a goldfish to go round the back of the waltzers to show off his bell end.

The parks are set on a 500 acre site around 30 miles south east of LA as the Disney crow flies. As you'd expect, there are 100's of hotels and motels within a few mile radius pouring out up to 50,000 excited Disney nerds every day ready for a day of expensive memories. With the recent opening of the new Star Wars Land, today promised to be very busy indeed.

We were excited and with bellies full of Lucky Charms, waffles, pancakes, cheese grits, donuts, steak n eggs (over easy) and a litre each of Gatorade, we waddled excitedly from "Mr Disney's Neighbour Hotel For The Poverty Stricken by Double Tree" to where it all began...

The very birthplace of the Disney Empire.

Stoked didn't do it justice.

(* not factually checked by me therefore do not eat the plants in Tomorrowland)

(** anecdotal, probably not true)

(*** not factually checked by me either therefore don't rely on anything in the following chapters as a guide to Disneyland California)

P.S. – Tropical storm with dry patches in Skibbereen

A Disney California Morning

Sponsored by Karma Krystals, Pasadena

As we walked alongside happy families, young couples and Disney nerds, we already had the sense that Disneyland California is a little more relaxed than Orlando. In a direct reflection of the good, stoned folk of California, the whole atmosphere seems to be very laid back - there was no manic rush to join the long, static queue when we reached the gates at opening time and no jostling to be first at rope drop. Just lots of people all waiting for the same thing with no-one trying to edge forwards or tutting if someone arrived late and joined their family further down the line.

Again, a bit like most of California it's also a little "funkier". I found that this has a creeping effect on you, the easy-going nature seeping into your psyche without knowing. I'd only been here a week or so and I was already wearing my cap backwards, going everywhere in flip flops and wearing a Tommy Bahama shirt. I was seriously thinking of jacking it all in, getting a pet monkey and busking a ukulele on Muscle Beach.

With not a cloud in the bright blue sky, we joined a few thousand people in the early morning sunshine, and we all edged as one toward the security check. Everyone took their time, and the staff were super friendly – joking with guests and making the little kids laugh with funny faces or taking the mick out of their parents.

Disney staff are ace, aren't they?

Just the happiest, nicest people doing a job they love. What a life, working in one the most Magical, happiest places on earth.

I'm struggling to think of another job where the staff are so permanently happy and upbeat. I'll have a think and let you know.

I say "security check" ... it wasn't so they could look for concealed weapons or contraband snacks so much as they could check your vibe and make sure you were cool enough to be chilled throughout the day. They only beep when someone goes through with a negative aura and they only frisk you to make sure you have a fresh tattoo, hipster beard and a spare bandana.

And that's just the kids.

We both set off the anxiety scanner and were asked to move to one side where a friendly looking counsellor was waiting for us, ready with some healing crystals that would check our chakras were balanced.

After a little while spent persuading them that we weren't tense, just British, they packed us off with a comfort box including Princess Jasmine scented candles, a Donald Duck stress ball and a pack of Goofy "herbal" fags called Shucks.

Isn't it legal to smoke weed in California? Or is the law that you MUST smoke weed in California? I get mixed up with that one.

Security done; we were now in line for the actual gates that heralded the entrance to Mr Disney's Californian Lair.

(Baby Tickler. That would be the happiest job in the world. According to Google, Disney staff aren't even in the top 10 of happiest professions but dental hygienists are. What a load of bollocks Google is sometimes).

Bizarrely, right at the front of the queue was a guy wearing a Wolverhampton Wanderers shirt. I said "orrlroight aer kid" and recognising a Black Country brother we instantly struck up a lengthy conversation that baffled those around us.

When us Black country folk get gewwin' most people think we're speaking a foreign language, like Dutch or Oirish.

This seems to happen to me a lot. No matter where I am in the world, from Shanghai to San Francisco or Malaysia to Miami, I'll guarantee that I'll overhear someone saying "Haa much?" in an exasperated Dudley accent and make an instant friend as we complain about the cost of everything, the funny food and the new bypass around Bilston

We are a breed apart, us Black Country folk. It must be the only area in the UK that issues its citizens with an emergency travel kit when they go abroad, to be used in extreme circumstances such as an earthquake, terrorist attack or a poor selection of real ale.

Each kit contains a vacuum pack of faggots and peas, a can of Banks's Bitter and a bag of scratchings. If you're from one of the few posh bits, like Stourbridge, you get a deluxe kit that includes one long-life turnip, a patterned, oily neckerchief and a Black Country to English dictionary.

When you meet a fellow Yam Yam (*) abroad, the tradition is to share some of your travel kit and have a good moan. The consequences of failing to carry this kit when confronted can be quite severe, ranging from a month's community service sweeping the streets of West Bromwich or picking the corn plasters out of the chlorinated sheep dip at Dudley Baths.

The harshest penalty I've ever heard for a repeat offender was a bloke who went unprepared on a "round the world" cruise. He met new Yam Yams at each port who tipped off the Black Country Elders –he returned home in shame and got banished to Cannock.

(* the nickname for an inhabitant of the Black Country, so-called after our predilection to shorten the words "*you are*" to "*yam*". This was invented as a piss take by a Brummie but now we proudly own it. In turn, we call Brummies, "pricks". Not affectionately.)

Me and my new mucka opened a pack of emergency scratchings and had a quick chinwag about Wolves new midfield formation and how it was "too bloody hot, aer kid". After a few lovely minutes spent chewing the fat, the crowd started to move forward so we bid each other a "tara a bit" just as the shutters went up on a new Disney day.

We were in!

The compulsory photo inside the gates was followed by a brisk mince towards the new "Star Wars Land". This had opened not that long ago in a meteor comet afterburner blaze of publicity, and we were keen to get there early on to see for ourselves.

It was no surprise to learn that we weren't the only ones with the same idea so there was a special rope drop just at the entrance, separating us mere mortals from the "Galaxy". We huddled together in excited anticipation with the Star Wars theme tune piped in via speakers hidden in bushes.

From our position we had a glimpse of the new land and could just about see all the staff getting ready – the Storm Troopers were getting their white plastic kit on, a very tall bloke was being helped into a Wookie costume and a dwarf in a white cape with big ears and a thyroid problem was having a green spray tan.

Now, I have a confession to make right here and now. I am not a Trekkie. Try as I might, I just don't get it and although I can see the appeal to nerds, geeks and socially awkward people who feel the need to fill their empty lives by being someone else in a pretend world and dress up like aliens, I'm afraid it's not for me.

In saying that, even I got excited with the hype surrounding this fantastic, expensive recreation of a Star Wars land and the much heralded state of the art new ride "Smugglers Run".

That is, until we did it.

No spoilers here folks, but if multi-million-dollar, underwhelming disappointment is your thing, then this is the awful ride for you!

Well worth you and your non-plussed girlfriend dressing up as Han Solo and Chewiebacca in 100 degrees and queuing two hours, to be jolted around for 3 minutes in a dimly lit bean can where you and your fellow "crew" can see fuck all, have no idea what's going on or what you're supposed to be doing.

Well done 21st century Disney Imagineers, you really nailed that one! Old Walt would be turning in his grave if he hadn't been cremated.

Anyway, like I say, no spoilers.

We alighted from our alien starship disappointment and had a bimble around Star Trek Land to try and find something else of interest to justify the two hours of our lives we'd lost standing in a boiling hot queue and melting my hair gel.

There wasn't.

But that's more of a reflection on me as a non-Star Wars fan so if all the alien stuff and pretend galaxy stuff puts your bins out, please go and have a look yourself. Live long and prosper my weirdo friend.

In the end, cos it was soooo hot, we settled for a mooch around the shops and some ice-cold refreshments. Sat on a wall, we heard the unmistakable sound of the Imperial Death March and looked up see Jacob Rees Mogg and his family had arrived, followed by some gay sounding storm troopers marching up and down scaring the shit out of little kids.

(Just changing the subject dead quick, Missus H struggles with names and words occasionally, examples of which will be repeated throughout this book for comedy value. Hence, we don't call them Storm Troopers on account that Missus H couldn't remember their name so just blurted out the first jumble of phonetically similar words that come into her head that's remotely close – in the Hadley house they're now and forever known as Troom Stoopers. This is also the reason that Peaky Blinders is Picky Flicks. And when Ant and Dec go to the Jungle, they don't do Bush Tucker trials – they do Bookafush Trials. More of that later).

We decided to go to warp speed and zoom out of Star Trek land in search of something more interesting, like the nearest library or some paint that's drying.

On the way out, we passed the newly arrived nerds dressed as Princess Leah, Luke Skywalker and Captain Spock, just as I was finishing my $15.00 C3PO brain freeze slushy.

I went over to shove it in the recycling bin, only to realise I'd try to lift the lid up on a little man dressed as R2D2.

I apologised profusely and bid him "may the force be with you" as Missus H hid from me and tried to latch on to a Latin American family all dressed as Wookies.

On to the rest of the park and we certainly crammed it in over the next few hours. We decided to do as much as possible given the fact that we'd paid Walt a small fortune for the privilege of our company so burnt the soles off our new "his n hers" Skechers and fairly raced around Critter Country and New Orleans Square, dearly wishing we had more time.

*****

No visit to the first of Mr Disney's Psycho Parks could possibly be complete without a go on It's A Small World, or, as Missus H calls it, It's A Crack House.

I LOVE **LOVE LOVE** It's A Small World. I don't care what anyone says, I think it's ace and a real triumph of what mankind can achieve with lots of spare time, MDF and a monster sized supply of mind bending drugs.

Apparently, the California one is bigger, weirder and more whacky (who would have guessed!) than the others, as demonstrated by the slightly different set pieces inside. I couldn't wait to get strapped in and see it for myself so we skipped to Fantasyland to find, quite unbelievably I know, there was **no queue**!

Wowser!

In giddy excitement, we were aboard in no time and set sail through the highly bleached waters, heading for miniature doll shenanigans and humorous adventure.

The United States diorama was first and totally different to the Orlando one, with just California represented by a stoner on a surfboard being chased by bears and sharks, whilst a fat little yellow haired in a blue suit and red cap doll danced around and then did a poo on copies of the constitution.

The other lands had an update too, in line with the ever-changing geo-political world. (And here's you expecting a book about Disney...? HA!).

Scotland had a little ginger lady doll, spouting racist abuse and repeatedly cleaving the border at Hadrians Wall with a pickaxe, while the rest of Britain's dolls ignored her and had a mass brawl amongst themselves.

Ireland looked on in exasperation with a little gay leprechaun saying "Lads, wat de absolute fuck are ya doin?"

Iran was testing a new batch of lethal looking fireworks, Mexico was separated from the US by a big new wall with half its inhabitants building ladders, France had a load of dolls in Yellow Vests throwing smoke bombs at the police and in Hong Kong everyone was dressed in black burning Chinese flags.

Most interestingly, half way round the ride somewhere in the Middle East, we came to a dead stop and hundreds of little dolls swam to empty boats, getting off in Germany to a warm welcome from half of the locals.

The ride reached a crescendo as we turned the final corner to be greeted by a whole host of dolls, all dressed in white and gold and absolutely belting out the theme tune that I won't repeat as it's probably already in your head. Amazingly, the actual, real life Greta Thunberg was in the middle of the choir! Talk about commitment. Thought she'd be too busy being a nuisance to Donald Trump or gluing herself to the side of an oil tanker.

But, the best thing of all, It's A Small World (or, IASW as us fans like to call it) only has it's OWN GIFT SHOP!

I KNOW!! How good is that?

I could have gone mad buying stuff but I'd spent all my holiday money on a Star Wars fanny pack. Otherwise, I would have had definitely forked out for the IASW ears, IASW fridge magnets or the IASW drain rod kit.

I did offer to get Missus H the extended vinyl version of the IASW theme tune, but she's already got a plastic 12 inch.

In the end, Missus H went over to the lovely girl behind the till, Loossee-Lou Nebraska, and brought me a souvenir t shirt which says, "I Conquered It's A Small World". I proudly wear it each and every day.

I'm wearing it now.

We moseyed on down to another favourite place of mine, Frontierland. As per the hilarious part in a previous chapter, you'll know that I've developed a thing for all things country and western since we first started to visit Orlando a few years back.

Maybe I was a cowboy in a previous life.

I love the smell of smoking meat (not a euphemism) and really fancied some sweet, sticky ribs. This didn't go down well with Missus H as she's never got over the trauma of seeing me eat a huge rack of em at TGI Fridays on a posh night out in Birmingham. I somehow managed to get more on me than in me and when I finished my chops were the colour of a surgeons gloves.

Missus H doesn't eat a lot so in the end we decided to share one of those "combo" type meals at The Golden Horseshoe that comes with unlimited salad, unlimited coke and unlimited indigestion.

Then on to Splash Mountain (not a toilet euphemism), Brer Rabbits Turnip Patch and finally Pooh Corner (that IS a toilet euphemism – my black-eyed peas were on the way back).

We couldn't stay here much longer as it was getting on for mid-afternoon and we had the entire other park to witness so with tired feet and full bellies we headed over for some more fun.

P.S. - Top marks if you didn't believe me and Googled "happiest profession".

P.P.S – No internet so couldn't check the weather in Skibbereen.

A Disney California Afternoon and Evening

Sponsored by Walt himself

Hello old friend, nice to see you again. You join us at the start of our journey around Disney California Adventure Park, which is the o*riginal* park.

This was quite a moment for me – I know I'm a cynical old git and poke fun at anything and everything at every opportunity but secretly I'm a big melt when it comes to nostalgia, and walking through the gates with my beautiful wife on a glorious sunny day in California made me realise just how lucky I am.

Even if we only had one day, it was still worth every dime just to be here. And it wasn't lost on me at all that we were in the original Disneyland Park and the only one to be built by old Walt himself.

I wondered what he would think if he could see it now.

I wondered what he'd make of the multibillion dollar he'd inadvertently created and the millions of lives he's touched.

I wondered what he'd make of all these happy families making lifelong memories and choffing on those big turkey legs at $20 each.

It's quite remarkable that he's achieved so much considering he's been dead for over 50 years.

We took it all in – the smells, the noise, and that special atmosphere you only get on a Disney day.

The only thing missing was the kids, something that we'd both acknowledged early on at breakfast (this was the first time we'd been on Disney property as parents without them) but secretly tried to keep a lid on our emotions for fear of a bubble snot meltdown.

Which inevitably came soon after on hearing the theme tune from Monsters Inc. as we walked towards "Pixar Pier", and it really hit us that we were here without our own little Woody and Jessie.

I've mentioned in the previous books that the Pixar films, especially Toy Story, Finding Nemo and Up, have a very special place in our hearts as they have indirectly provided a backdrop to our married life and the kids growing up. The songs, the characters and stories have been benchmarks for lots of different times in our family life. They all have their own meaning, and it makes my heart swell and tears form just at the thought of my now grown up children as little dots in pushchairs.

It's quite incredible how that makes me feel and I wish I could do all that again. I spent waaaay too much time working and missed out on a lot of the kids growing up, thinking it was more important to earn money than be at home being a good dad.

If you're a parent of a little kid reading this, hug them close for me and please soak up every single minute of their little existence before they do what mine did and grow into big, mouthy lumps.

And if you're a young dad and you know you're working too much, stop it. Trust me on this brother, it's not worth it.

Pixar Pier is wonderful. You enter under an old-fashioned arch, bedecked in pretty, colourful fairground lights, one side of which spells out one of the slogans from "Up"

"*Adventure is out there*".

It is a nod back to Walt's original vison of a 1930's style fairground with marquee tents, a giant ferris wheel with a huge Mickey face in the middle and rootin tootin arcade games. There are four separate neighbourhoods all surrounding a big manmade lake full of crocodiles — Incredibles Park, Toy Story Boardwalk, Pixar Promenade and Inside Out Headquarters.

We drifted around each part. We played games on Toy Story Boardwalk, toured above the park on the strangely named "Pixar Pal A Round"

Ferris wheel and looped the loop on the Incredicoaster.

I'm sure I'm not alone in thinking this but isn't the costume for Mrs Incredible just a bit too sexy?

I'm not complaining mind – I think she looks great and them long arms would be a real bonus getting stuff down from the loft. (By the way lads, I've checked and you can get the outfit for your missus. It's not official Disney merch though. Just go to www.pervertscosplay.com)

I loved the fact that unlike Orlando Disney it pays homage to the other less celebrated Pixar productions, giving much deserved attention to some films that are brilliantly written, superbly crafted but don't share the limelight with the box office smashers. One of these is Inside Out, and another on the list that can reduce me to tears in an instant. If you know this line from the character Bing Bong, you'll know exactly what I mean:

"Take her to the moon for me, ok?"

I've just typed that through tears. God I'm such a wuss.

At the end of Pixar Pier is a spinny type ride dedicated to the film called "Inside Out Emotional Whirlwind". Given our delicate state of mind and my even more delicate stomach after stuffing my face with Woody's Churros, we decided to give this one a miss.

We spent a few hours at Pixar Pier, having decided that it was a better to soak up and enjoy one part of the park rather than rush around and miss things. And because it gives us an excuse to come back one day and see the bits we've missed.

Eventually we ambled out and headed over to a new spot I hadn't seen on the map called Stoners Corner. Always one for keeping up with the zeitgeist, Walt has created a very fitting and realistic section of his Psycho Park dedicated to one of California's best-known pastimes – getting higher than a NASA satellite.

It's a real hip little zone that includes Gastons Grow Shop, Eeyores Edibles and Mary Janes Mazin' Milkshakes. Beanbags have replaced benches and both Bobs Dylan and Marley were being pumped through speakers disguised as gigantic ganja plants.

There was a lovely, relaxed vibe with mums and dads losing all sense of reason and responsibility, tittering away while their kids ran amok. One dad was smiling and giggling whilst his toddler climbed over the fence to the crocodile filled lake.

"Go on Solstice, my lil champ. They won't bite you my baby superman…. You've seen Captain Hook"

114

Conscious of the time, I rescued Missus H as she shared a doobie with a young gay couple called Chip Munk and Butter Cup and we sniggered off for more adventures.

We rattled around as much as we could in the remaining hours of daylight, given that we were stone tired. We knew we wanted to see the famous light show at kicking out time so made the decision to spend the last bit of our day in another new area to us – Cars Land.

Cars doesn't have the same draw as other Pixar films for me. Maybe it's because it's what I do (sort of) for a living or maybe it's because it's less believable than the other films. I mean, the whole concept is ridiculous, say compared to real life toys or fish that can talk.

Nevertheless, we'd heard good things and looked forward to meeting Mater and the gang.

We were not disappointed. Cars Land is quite possibly one of the nicest areas in all the theme parks I've been to (and that's saying something as it includes the canal wharf at The Black Country Museum where they film Peaky Blinders / Picky Flicks).

The whole area is fab – themed on Radiator Springs, it is immaculately put together with great rides and interesting shops full of different tat that we'd not seen before. There's an old school café called Flo's V8 Diner, an Italian car garage called Luigis and an utterly fabulous spinning teacups type ride called Maters Junkyard Jamboree. Billed as a "toe tapping, tractor spinning thrill ride" it is absolutely hilarious and we had a real out of body, pee-your-pants moment as we were hurled from one direction to the next Mater singing to a hick tune with a picky banjo. Not bad for a middle-aged couple on a kids ride.

The very last ride we managed was possibly the best though – the Radiator Springs Racers. This is fabulous too, especially as we did it in the dark, and the only other ride I've been on where you see actual skidmarks - the other being the first time I went on Rip Ride Rockit. You're strapped in to one of two colourful race cars and zoom off around a Scalextric type track with a backdrop identical to the mountainous range in the Cars movie. It was a fantastic way to end our park tour and another reason why we want to go back.

Our mega busy day ended with the spectacular light show in the heart of the park called World Of Color. They manage to get all the crocodiles to bed before setting up the lighting rigs in the lake with the enormous Mickey ferris wheel and fairground providing a stunning backdrop. Thousands of us gathered together under a darkening sky, just as all the lights were dimmed for greater effect and a sweet Disney tune lifted the sense of excitement.

I'm going all mushy again but it really is a Disney masterpiece – it combines amazing water effects, a booming, emotional soundtrack and an astounding light show. It really needs to be seen to be believed – how they manage to project a near perfect film on to the back of a huge waterfall, whilst timed precisely with an incredible light show is astonishing.

Each song and film accompanies a different soundtrack, each one weaving a story that makes you laugh one second and cry the next.

I'm lucky enough to have seen the light shows and fireworks in several different parks now but this was far and away the best I'd ever seen.

Go and Google it now and you'll see what I mean. Well, after you've finished this chapter obvs – there's a only a few lines left so that would be quite rude.

It left both Missus H and I in tears and we just stood and hugged each other for a good few minutes after it finished, sobbing at the end of a very happy and emotional day.

Clever buggers these Disney folk. They know precisely the right moment to make you laugh, astound you and to tug at your heart strings. And the California Disneyland light show does exactly that – go see for yourself.

And that was that. We trudged back to the "Pretend Disney Motel for the Financially

Deprived" very happy and very tired. Our first parent Disney trip without kids had been an emotional rollercoaster but we proved that we are still just big kids ourselves and able to have just as much fun without them. We had laughed, cried and got stoned together and made the most of a truly awesome day.

Walt would be proud.

Next stop – Orlando!

A trip across country and... Orlando!

Sponsored by Stolichnaya Vodka

After several long days working and our one day in Disneyland California, it was now time for us to kick back, relax and get our holiday underway. Well, if there is such a thing as kicking back and relaxing on an Orlando holiday – all previous holidays to the Sunshine State have been like a bootcamp with Mouse ears.

The only downside to this that is does mean a very long flight across country. Not sure if you know this but America is proper massive, and we were flying from the left(ish) bit down to the bottom right bit. It would have cost a fortune in an Uber.

We were flying at 7 in the morning and as I like to get to the airport nice and early to snaffle vodka rations from duty free, I gave Missus H a cup of coffee and a cheeky bum nudge about 03.30. After a few moments of disorientated mumblings where she asked Molly to jump up on the bed and reminded me to put the bins out, she reluctantly sat up.

She's not great in the morning, Missus H. She loves a lie in and takes a long time to come round to the idea of getting up and starting the day. Not helped by me being the total opposite – once I'm awake, I'm up, stomping around the place like a baby elephant, opening squeeky wardrobe doors and inadvertently switching on the lamp that's just above her face.

I decided against watching any more American TV as I get to distracted by the insane adverts (more of that later) as we needed to get going so once we'd showered, rammed everything into our massive bags and said goodbye to the room, we chucked all of our gear in an Uber and headed to the airport through the still sleeping city.

My usual pre-flight routine of getting higher than a hippy in an air balloon was interrupted somewhat by the fact that we flew at 7 in the morning, meaning no bars were open in the airport. And I'd now realised that even though this flight was 6 hours long, we were only flying from one bit of America to another – which meant no Duty Free!

It was time to execute Plan B, which involves cracking into the emergency supply of vodka hidden in those little 100 ml travel bottles that you get from Superdrug. I've got 2, one marked as "Conditioner" and the other in a mini spray bottle that looks like a de-mister. I also ask Missus H to take a couple through security in her Ziploc bag just in case one of us gets stopped. It worked a treat today and after a few milligrams of a Happy Horsey Pills washed down with a cocktail of apple juice and vodka flavoured skin conditioner, I quickly morphed into the dopier version of myself needed to tackle the thought of being strapped into a big metal pipe with wings that don't flap.

As my brain swirled around inside my drunken head, I vaguely recall stumbling to the gate with my laces undone and Missus H asking me to stop pointing and singing "It's A Small World After All" to a dwarf in the queue to board the plane.

The dwarf overheard me and turned round to quite rightly call me out, putting me firmly in my place. There then followed an exchange that I'm not proud off:

Dwarf: "Excuse me sir, I find your tone and sense of humour outrageous. I insist you stop right now."

Me: "Why? Is it belittling you?"

Dwarf: "Really!! That demonstrates your total lack of understanding and ignorance. What do you know about dwarves?"

Me: "Very little..."

And with that, Missus H gave me a swift kick to the shin, apologised to the dwarf and begged forgiveness on the grounds of my drunken, stupid state. Which worked, as she's good like that and a few moments later we were on the plane and I fell fast asleep.

I must be a joy to fly with.

We arrived in Orlando mid-afternoon, compared to California where it was windy and a little chilly, it was hot.

Baking hot.

So hot in fact I had to open all the windows and eventually take my clothes off – much to the surprise of the Magical Express driver and the other families on board.

For the first few days of this mental, physical and financial endurance test, we're getting our Mickey fix by staying at one of the posher properties on Mr Disney's real estate list – The Beach Club Hotel. It's situated on a complex that includes the neighbouring Yacht Club, The Boardwalk and two non-Disney properties called Swan and Dolphin.

The hotels surround a man-made lake full of crocodiles that has Epcot at one end and Hollywood Studios at t'other. All along the lake, old style Disney ferry boats bob along the water transporting folk from park to park, generally manned by crusty old blokes who probably never dreamed that one day in their fifties they would be wearing a little sailor boy outfit for a living and in charge of a machine that can be controlled by one single lever that only goes forwards or backwards.

Just in front of The Boardwalk hotel itself there is an actual boardwalk – a long, wide sweeping promenade that circles the main part of the lake and has a collection of expensive restaurants, takeaways and old-fashioned family entertainment, all set against a backdrop of pastel coloured New England style buildings.

It's especially pretty at night, with cute fairy lights all along The Boardwalk illuminating the picturesque backdrop. And there's less kids.

We've stayed at The Beach Club before (see book 1) – it's a very nice place to stay with loads of old-fashioned decoration, relics and memorabilia in a sort of pseudo "Olde Worlde" nautical theme. Almost like a retirement home for old sailors without the smell of wee, cabbage or fish.

Safely checked in at the Beach Club, where we also collected our Magic Bands that had been pre-loaded with all of our vital details like Fast Pass plans, dining reservations and monthly disposable income, we hoisted our cases up to our room and decided to make a plan for the rest of the day. We were in two minds to just stay by the pool for a few hours before dinner, but in the end plumped for a few hours over in Epcot. This was because of two things:

1) I'd paid for the park tickets and I was determined to get my money's worth, and

2) I'd been talked into getting the Dining Plan by the tele-sales girl at Disney, Cherrabelle Nebraska, even though we were only staying a few days. The Dining Plan starts from the day you arrive and as it was now around 5 o clock, I'm technically behind and therefore losing money.

So, not wanting to miss a thing and to try and get value for money, we boot scooted over to Epcot and our first "Quick Service" meal on the Disney Dingo Dollar All You Can Scoff Dining Plan.

I've been on this dining plan a few times now, and I still have absolutely <u>no</u> idea whatsoever how it works.

I appreciate that some of you may not be familiar with this, or be aware of the intricacies of this comprehensive culinary plan – a bit like not knowing how to calculate say, the load sheet of a Boeing 747, or why the BBC think that The Kumars at No. 42 is funny.

The basic concept is that you give Mr Disney half your pension and in return he gives you "credits" per person per day for the duration of your stay.

Credits are in the shape of:

Snacks (stuff that comes in a packet with a use by date of 2030)

Quick Service Meals (meals you eat with your own hands or wobbly plastic cutlery) or

Table Service Meals (waited service where you're served by smiley girls called Krystall or Bethanee Lollipop-Jayne who have <u>far</u> too much happiness in their life and expect an extra 20% tip just for doing their job properly).

There's also an upgrade to The Dumbo Deluxe Disney Dingo Dollar Dining Plan, where for just a few thousand dollars more you can get double the food allowance, a free defibrillator and a crash cardiac arrest team on speed dial.

Successful holiday makers who complete either of Mr Disney's "Scoff Til You Drop" plans get a special voucher to claim a 20% discount of a home stomach stapling kit available from Bath and Bodyworks at Disney Springs.

I think that's how it works... I'll keep you posted.

We headed into Epcot through the back door (The Beach Club is located just behind Epcot, a short crocodile swim down the lake) and first off we had a little stroll around the UK. It's been a while since we were at Epcot and the UK has evidently had a makeover by the Disney Imagineers to keep it up to date.

The "Olde Worlde Gift Shoppe" selling Peter Rabbit crockery, expensive fudge and Arran sweaters has been replaced by "The Village

Vaporium" vape shop, the fish and chip stall has gone and is now "Mushaq's Chicken Lickin' Shack" and the spot where they used to have the Toy Pavilion is now a Poundland.

Most surprisingly, The Rose and Crown has recently undergone a multi-hundred pound makeover and just re-opened as an Aldi.

Before we got too nostalgic, and cos we were getting hungry after smelling Mushaq's chicken, we decided to pop our Dining Plan cherry with a Quick Service meal.

But, where to go? There's such a wide and varied choice for your indigestion here at Epcot and we couldn't agree on what we wanted. Missus H wanted to walk all the way to Germany for her favourite "Schnitzle in Apfelwein" – she doesn't eat a lot but every time we come here she always wants pork in cider.

I was dying to go back to North Korea and try the new restaurant, "Kim Jong-Ungry". Trust me, if you get a chance, go to Kim's – everything on the menu is superb but the meatballs are the dogs bollocks.

In the end, we compromised and agreed on tasty noodles so made our way through the early evening crowds packed with bored kids and pissed up parents waiting for the fireworks (well, let's face it gang - that's all Epcot is, isn't it?) and headed toward China and "Poo Ping's Takeaway".

Well it was a Saturday and if we were at home we'd be having this in front of any one of the thousands of shite programmes featuring Ant and Dec. We get our noodles from "Yu Wha", a takeaway run by a deaf bloke from Beijing.

We queued for ages at the counter to place our order. The sweet but extremely short-sighted Chinese girl on the till was struggling with the buttons on the register, getting increasingly agitated as she furiously stabbed at each button, followed by a string of exasperated Chinese profanities (I know this cos I can speak Chinese. Honest).

In an attempt to help, I smiled gently at her and in my best Dudlaay / Chinese accent asked if she was ok in Mandarin.

Her name was Ping, and she explained she'd only been put on the tills today as she was causing too much confusion in the kitchen by shouting "What?" every time the microwave went off.

I helped her to press the buttons on the till, and five minutes later ended up with crispy chicken's feet, duck's gizzard and a side of pork intestines. Yum.

Missus H settled for house special curry with extra mushrooms, half rice / half chips.

With satisfied burps and the rather worrying start of localised chaffing to my inner thighs, we shuffled back to The Beach Club for $15.00 gin and tonic nightcap to see off the end of a packed first day.

And so to bed.

P.S. – earth tremor in Skibbereen.

A Magical day at Hollywood Studios

This chapter is bought to you by our new sponsor, Lady Liniment, the all-new improved balm to help soothe the burn of localised lady chafing.

This chub rub isn't exclusive to you women ya know...

It happens to us men too, even the hunky ones like me, but we just don't feel the need to talk about the intricacies of our nether regions on Facebook groups. I reckon I've found a cure for it though so feel free to discuss the following with your Orlando Facebook friends and make sure you tell this to your own Grumpy too - ***bamboo boxer shorts***!

My God they're good. I'll never forget that heavenly first time I pulled on my first pair, cupping my tackle and sliding them smoothly up and over my pert buttocks – it was majestic; like diving into a swimming pool on a hot day or discovering the tasty delight of scratchings all over again.

They are as light as a feather, dead comfy and grip in all the right areas, if you know what I mean. Smooth to the touch, they have the added bonus of the elasticated ability to accentuate size and length, meaning that even ickle Tom Cruise would look like Usain Bolt. Or, in my case, my

Greggs sausage roll looks like a Dunelm Mills bolster cushion.

However, given that God put men's dangly bits in the place where they are most likely to get damp, crinkly and sweaty, every so often you will still need to adjust yourself to prevent the old "flying squirrel". Easily done though by performing a first position pliet, followed by a quick shuffle ball change (jazz hands optional).

I knew all those ballet and tap lessons would come in handy one day. Thanks mum x.

Despite the early onset of chub rub, we were both really excited about today and our first full day in our absolute favourite park, Hollywood Studios. Which was going to be strange without the kids around, but we were determined to make the most of our new-found, non-child freedom.

And even though it is just the two of us, the actual routine on a park day is still quite stressful. I've experienced this before and I have to admit it was me being the pushy one when we were here with the kids.

I guess I'm not alone in this as Orlando holidays do seem to bring out the stress in everyone. Almost from the minute you wake up you're already worrying about being late – getting stuck behind thousands of better prepared fams in the entrance queue and then even more of them to get on your favourite ride. Your whole early morning demeanour takes on a new, heightened sense of anxiety as you upset everyone by rushing yourself, husband / wife, kids through ablutions, getting dressed and not eating breakfast just to save ten minutes.

When you think about it, it's not really worth it, is it?

I was determined not to stress about rushing to get out but we did set our alarms early today as it was "Extra Magic Hours" at Hollywood Studios. For those of you that don't know, "Extra Magic Hours" is an ingenious idea that Mr Disney came up with to get more people to stay in his hotels; namely, get punters to pay to stay in a property he owns in exchange for giving them an extra hour in a psycho park he also owns before the non-Disney riff-raff turn up.

The extra hour means that he can get you to buy more tat in a park that you've already paid to get in... It really is very clever when you think about it.

As per usual, I was awake and up well before Missus H and after my morning ritual of stretches, joint cracks and moans, set to a soundtrack of quite incredible farts of varying length and tone which seemed to be perfectly timed to each grumpy step, I did battle with the dreaded American coffee machine to ultimately present her with a lukewarm plastic cup of caffeine-packed fluid whilst standing in front of her still half-asleep with my willy poking out of my Eeyore pyjamas.

That's one of the best sentences I've ever written.

She eventually came to and, after realising where she was, patted my willy back in, sat up and started to chat excitedly about the day ahead. She drained her coffee and did a quick level on Candy Crush before we both set about our morning routine in readiness to beat the massive queue at "rope drop". Ever the gentleman, I take care of all the important stuff in the preparation – the essential stuff like Magic Bands, park maps, phone chargers, credit cards, cash... and the half bottle of vodka smuggled in with the Minute Maid apple juice.

This leaves Missus H with just one thing to sort out.

Only one thing... but it is a crucial thing. One that is of such vital importance to our shared enjoyment that it can pretty much make or break our day... It is the big question:

"Hair up, or hair down?"

I hate this question. It is in the same category as "Does this bag go with these shoes?" or "Does this dress make me look like mutton?"

I have a 50 / 50 chance of getting this right.

Me: "Hair down. It looks nice"

... is the wrong answer!

I don't know why she ever asks me these questions as I obviously don't know... It'd be easier to knit spaghetti than second guess what she's thinking.

Fifteen minutes later, with hair up in a construction of grips, bobbles, slides, pins and scrunchies to create an effect that Gaudi would be proud of, off we marched in the beautiful early morning sunshine to Hollywood Studios and a date with Slinky Dog in Toy Story Land.

As suspected, and despite arriving a whole thirty minutes before the park officially opened, we joined the back of a queue that was at least a thousand strong – or an extra one and a half hours wait for Slinky, whichever way you look at it.

This was not a pleasant experience, dear reader. We were sort of corralled into a big, horrible, heaving mass of sweaty human beings and made to wait in the full, baking hot sunshine. There was no shade and no way you could leave the queue without losing your spot. Each time I looked behind me the body of people just seemed to get bigger and bigger and bigger.

"Magic Hour" it was not.

The queue was a right mixture of excited folk but with a heavy concentration of Military Mums, along with their brow beaten hubbies and her private little infantry who had obviously been ready since 8 o clock last night.

You'll never beat a Military Mum – the precision that goes into the planning is quite incredible, with sharpened, pointy elbows, coloured and laminated schedules, pre-planned dining times and every provision that you will <u>ever</u> need for <u>any</u> eventuality.

Military Mums with the big buggies are next level, mind. I'm sure those big buggies are just being used for bashing people out of the way and carrying "Emergency Mum Supplies", say in case there was an outbreak of bird flu just after the kids had met Donald, Mr Disney ran out of Pinot Grigio or a fellow Military Mum called out in distress and needed spare Valium.

We stood patiently for a while in the hot queue until eventually a Cast Member called Duke Bo-Diddley Jr decided it was safe for us to be let go and allowed us to head off en masse towards Toy Story Land and everyone's new favourite, the Slinky Dog ride.

And that's where it got a little crazy... I knew we were going to be emotional and I knew it was going to be busy, but the combination of the two and the fact that it was hotter than a jalapeño fart meant for an uncomfortable hour or so spent simultaneously queuing and melting with a load of equally tense fellow holiday makers just to ride a dog.

** avoids temptation to make another infantile joke involving dogs and West Bromwich **

In the end, it took us around an hour or so to get on, and it was well worth the wait. It's real fun, with interesting stuff to look at while you're in the queue and a rip-roaring, stomach bouncing ride at the end. The main premise of the ride is that you're on Slinky's back as he races through Andy's back garden where there are loads of abandoned toys in the grass. We loved it and as soon as we walked off and the stress lifted, the emotion of being in Toy Story Land with no kids hit us.

As you may know from my previous ramblings, we both love all the Pixar stuff and it's probably the main reason for our love for Disney (and therefore, Orlando). Our kids have grown up with it and it's impossible to separate the films from their childhood. Every film, theme tune, special song or scene still leaves us both as emotional wrecks.

The beginning montage of Up! is a full on blarty, snot bubble crying meltdown, the "I love you, Dad" scene in Nemo has us both wailing like banshees and we had to have counselling after we watched the scene in Toy Story 3 where Andy hands his toys over to Bonnie. Get this - it came out on the SAME DAY that our eldest, Sam, left big school... It was horrendous, we were literally bawling in the cinema in Dudley, much to the total disgust of the kids. I could cry now just thinking about it.

The kids are sort of grown up now, so the Pixar magic was sort of wearing off... that was until a re-booted, bad ass Bo Peep turned up in Toy Story 4 as a tough, blonde Lara Croft type wearing a satin all in one outfit and carrying a bum-whacking instrument that, if you're a pervert, could easily be mistaken for a whip.

The introduction of Bo Peep MK II made it all a bit more interesting for the dads – a bit like when Herminyonny had a do-over in Harry Potter if you know what I mean.

They're not daft are they, this Pixar lot?

Need to find more reasons to engage a wider demographic and ensure dads get something out of a film?

Easy peasey, melons squeezy. Reintroduce a previously two-dimensional doll as a Diana Dors type buxom blonde urban warrior with attitude, shiny skin and a suedo-pervy accessory THEN sell the dressy up outfits in adult sizes at the theme parks to get the mums on board.

Genius move.

We loitered around the gift shop and they did have loads of sexy Bo outfits in stock, but not one that fitted me. They only go up to size 18 and, try as I might, I couldn't persuade Missus H to get one. I even tried to bribe her by giving her a little Woody, but as usual she was having none of it.

We spent ages in Toy Story land, soaking up the sunshine and deliberately sitting still up a corner to take it all in. You can do that when you've no kids and it was a bit of a revelation to us, the fact that you don't need to rush around and appreciate what's going on around you. It's amazing how much you miss, being in a rush.

For example, we stood (then sat) and watched the Green Soldiers twice. These guys are incredibly entertaining and managed to put in two really funny, original performances even though they were covered from head to toe in almost 100-degree heat. They take the mickey out of themselves, the mums and dads and especially the little kids and although the jokes are a bit corny it's absolutely brilliant entertainment.

The other thing you notice when you stop still is just how much joy Disney brings to kids, and sometimes the joy etched on a little child's face when they see Woody or Jessie is truly magical.

I feel the same when I see Nigella Lawson.

We managed to find some shade in the queue for the spinny Buzz's Alien Teacups and then I got my butt kicked by Missus H in the rootin' tootin' shut-em-up Midway Mania game. I reckon I only lost cos my trigger was stuck and the gun wouldn't spin round. Think the bearings had gone... It's quite remarkable how many times that happens to me as I always lose to the kids on that other firing alley game. You know, the one with Buzz and Zurg where you have to shoot a 5 cm target from 20 feet with a rattly plastic gun as the kids spin you around. Can't remember what it's called...

Eventually we peeled ourselves away from the hot tarmac in Toy Story Land and headed to do the rest of the park. We both love Hollywood Studios and we pretty much did everything we wanted, including Star Tours, Indiana Jones, Singalonga Frozen (another blartfest) and Aerosmith. We got great seats at the back of the theatre for Beauty and the Beast so I could have a snooze and just before the heavens opened I managed to persuade Missus H to brave the Tower of Terror.

She hates this ride -it utterly terrifies her. And I admit, I was nervous about this too. But I guess that's sort of the reason for going on it; ya know, let out some of your adrenaline? I was also a little nervous that my lunch of burrito and black-eyed beans might reappear in my adrenaline so all through the scary queue I did my tightest buttock clench not to give the game away.

Despite having buttocks of steel, it all became a bit too much in the end and I don't mind admitting here dear reader that I let out quite a series of gufty trumps as the lift ascended to each floor, eventually dropping to earth in a brown cloud.

It was wrong on so many levels.

Buzz Lightyear's Space Ranger Spin. I just remembered.

Anyway, the day wouldn't be complete without a moan now would it? So here it is...

This was our first full park day in Orlando and as a result also our first experience of a huge volume of people. Sure, we'd spent the day at Disneyland California and a bop around Epcot yesterday evening, but both were tame compared to today. California was busy but chilled, and I can't remember a single incident where we nudged in a queue or any hassle as we walked. And as for Epcot yesterday... well, it's empty most the time cos it's a bit boring.

Aaaah, they were all out in force today; all the idiots that can't <u>decide</u> where they wanna go, the ones who have no idea <u>where</u> they wanna go, the ones who <u>know</u> where they wanna go and bash people out of the way or just the ones that are plain <u>stoopid</u>. Spotted em all on our travels - The Sudden Stoppers, The Change of Directioners,

The Dawdlers, The Map Readers... and of course, The Military Mums.

I covered this last time (in hilarious fashion too! You should really buy the other books) and a year on I reckon I have the answer to the problem. It's such an easy solution that I'm amazed that no-one has ever thought of it before. In fact, as soon as we got back to the hotel, I sat and wrote a letter to Mr Disney himself – carry on reading...

Our first park day ended with a ferry ride back to The Beach Club, followed by a 10,000 calorie, sit down, two course meal at the ESPN sports bar. Which was two credits. I think.

Both mains were enormous and probably more than enough for four people, never mind two. Add to that the fact that Missus H eats less than a sparrow in Winter so you can imagine how much was leftover.

We declined the offer of pudding until we realised it was included in the Dining Deal, so obviously had the two biggest ones so we could get our money's worth. (We had em "to go" and they were still in the fridge 3 days later).

We waddled back to our digs with full bellies, blistered feet and happy hearts, and despite the heat, the screaming kids and the crowds we had soaked up every minute and made the very most of a wonderful day.

Mr Walt Disney
The Big Castle
Magic Kingdom Theme Park
Orlando

Ref: Adults Only Magic Hours

Dear Mr Disney,

I hope you are well and business is good. I hope this is the right address to write to – I'm guessing that it is as I'm sure I've seen you popping your head out of the castle during the late-night fireworks display.

I spent a day with my missus in Hollywood Studios today and we had a great time an all that but man alive it was busy. It was just the two of us cos our kids have grown out of all the Disney nonsense (no offence, like) so you'd have thought it would have been easier to get around.

Hope you don't mind me saying but in my opinion you're letting <u>way</u> too many kids in the park. I know it's a family thing and a lot of the rides are about kids, but come on... getting a bit ridiculous now mate.

I love the idea of extra Magic Hours so you can get em spending early, and also cos it's a gnat's cock quieter, so I've come up with a belter of an idea to combine the two. You'll like this…

ADULTS ONLY MAGIC HOURS!!

Can you imagine? What a great idea, uh?

You could apply this to all your parks (especially Epcot, as adults only really go there to get pissed). Here's how I think it would shake down, obviously you and your team are free to add your own ideas:

1) At 12.00 each day, sound the *Enchanted Fanfare* (I'd suggest "*Bohemian Rhapsody*" by Oasis) and all children have to quietly leave the park for two hours * or put em in those germ free ball pits like they have at IKEA in Wednesbury.

* Big stroller families or families with 4 kids or more have to stay out for 3 hours.

2) Turn all the music down to an acceptable level where you can still listen to the music but hear yourself think.

3) Free alcohol, especially for adults that haven't bought any kids with them. They should get special recognition for doing their bit, like celebration t-shirts or gold Magic Bands.

4) Absolutely NO matching t shirts allowed during Adult Hours. Anyone found breaking this rule will be forced to swap their day in a good park for 3 days at Epcot.

5) No screaming, loud laughing and no running.

6) And, absolutely NO SUDDEN CHANGING OF DIRECTION. Everyone must be respectful of each other and walk at a steady, considered pace and stick to the direction your brain and eyes have chosen to head in.

7) No Candy Crushing or TikTok. Also applies to any on-line gambling app like the ones advertised during The Chase, such as Foxy Lotto, Bored Housewife Spinners or Gala Bingo Wings.

I'm amazed no-one has suggested this before to be honest and I reckon this is a goer. I even reckon with the right marketing you could charge extra money for this - just think of all that extra turnover! You can spend the extra cash on bigger ball pits when it takes off and maybe some better fireworks!

Look forward to hearing from you. I'm staying with the missus at The Beach Club til next Monday so if you want to swing by for a coffee and a chat, let me know.

Have a Magical day

Yours,

Disgruntled of Dudley

Michael Hadley

Laundry and a bit of Magic Kingdom Day

Proudly sponsored by Lenor

We decided to give our poor feet a rest today after yesterday's 22,000 hot step shuffle around Hollywood Studios, so after a Quick Service Breakfast of sausages, scrambled egg and a scone (?), our plan for today was to take it easy by The Beach Club pool whilst Missus H did the laundry in between some sunbathing.

Before we set off, Missus H asked me to "do me back…" which is shorthand for "come here buffoon and pleeeease try to get the right amount of suntan cream on me bits I can't reach. And don't be a perv about it".

Similar to my answers to such tricky marital questions I get asked such as the aforementioned "Hair up or down?", "Do these trainers match my foundation?" and "Do these jeans make me look short and stumpy?", the application of suntan cream on my wife's torso is something else that I never get right.

It's either too little or not enough, with too much in one place and nothing somewhere else. That's why her boobs never burn.

So, with me at the control of her semi naked body and a full tube of Aldi factor 30, she's either gonna burn or look like she's about to swim the channel.

I have no idea how much is enough, so I start with a handful of cream and a gentle wipe over the areas she's indicated, which results a few moments later in her checking in the mirror and shouting "You've missed a bit!" or "Do you <u>want</u> me to burn?"

I wind up to have another go, splodging a proper dollop into both hands and furiously rubbing it in like I'm buttering the Christmas turkey.

Which now is obviously too much.

And I admit I'm a bit clumsy so while half of it splatters on Mr Disney's floor, I end up patting the excess cream down like she's on fire while she sways from side to side like she's being shoved violently through a car wash, whilst moaning at me to stop holding her boobs in place.

Eventually, we reach a point where I'm happy cos I've copped a cheeky feel and she's satisfied that she's not gonna burn, although she does look like a human Chelsea Bun.

Ready for a bit of pool inaction and with a good few days of smelly laundry wrapped into one of Mr Disney's bath towels, off we popped downstairs headed for a place that still gives me the creeps from the last time we were here.

I'm gonna get into a lot of trouble for this, but

what is it with you lovely women and a holiday laundry? It's like some sort of sacred room where all of you abide by a set of secret rules – rules that have been handed down through maternal generation to generation, never to be shared with us useless men

I've said it before and I'll say it again - women utterly baffle me. And the one I live with in particular. The changes of mind, the mood swings, the hot and cold flushes... all of it is a total puzzle. And just when you think you've cracked it, the goalposts move. Or disappear altogether.

Here's one; Missus H has two pairs of brown, knee length boots similar to the ones worn by the cat in Shrek. One are called "Day Boots", the other "Night Boots" and she wears either pair depending on the time of day and where she's going.

When I asked why she's got two pairs of identical boots she looked at me like I was insane and replied "One pair make me look taller than the other".

I measured em - they are exactly the same.

But the holiday laundry is another level... stick any woman into a shared washroom area and all of a sudden they turn from a beautiful, soft, luscious, albeit baffling being into some sort of primeval warrior / dementor with Inspector

Gadget arms, ready to defend their families pile of soiled, sweaty, skid-marked garments as if their life depends on it.

The holiday laundry is no place for a man. We don't know how to operate those scary machines and we don't know how to fold properly. And no man on the planet knows the difference between bio or non-bio until he gets back home to find he's bought the wrong one.It's always the wrong one, no matter which one you buy.

And, unless you want your tongue pulled out, god forbid you should try to make small talk with another woman while she's sorting her undies out...

You may recall from book number one that I learnt this the hard way a few years ago when, by way of trying to help Missus H with our laundry, I removed another woman's washing from a machine... just as she walked in. She caught me holding her big knickers in one hand and her daughter's Elsa dress in the other and I swear if there'd been a baseball bat within reach I'd have been clubbed to death.

So I wasn't looking forward to this trip as Missus H's washing Sherpa so headed to the laundry with some trepidation, just in case she left me on my own to deal with one of them big white machines and I accidentally put my red Bob The Builder pyjamas in with her big white monthly pants. Again.

As it turned out, the laundry was empty save for another lovely holiday mum also from the UK, and with just a few nods, winks and secret words her and Missus H divided the machines and big folding table between them. Having never met before in their lives, within minutes they were best laundry buddies and I was given the nod that my services were no longer needed and I could go and play in the pool while the grown ups talked.

Which I did with absolute pleasure. And while I drifted around the lazy river drinking an early morning Bahama Breeze, Missus H simultaneously orchestrated a multitude of machines with her new best pal which eventually led to a fresh pile of my undergarments ready to be McQueened in no time.

Lovely.

*****

Later on in the afternoon we headed over to our first, and as it turned out only, trip to the Magic Kingdom, to be met with a throng of people the like of which I'd only ever seen at the Barry Manilow concert at Wembley back in 1984.

My god it was busy. We queued up for ages at bag check and then again at the fingerprint check in, where I mistakenly thought the lady cast member called Shareen Labelle was talking to me when she said "try again Princess" when my finger wouldn't register. I thought, that's odd, how does she know my safe word? Until I realised she was talking to a little girl next to me with grubby fingers.

Once inside, we were amazed by just how many people Mr Disney had let in today. Maybe takings were down recently so he'd decided to let a few extra thousand folk in to get his revenue up. We had a few Fast Passes for stuff, but every other ride or attraction had crazy-long queueing times – except for the Hall of Presidents, obviously. That only gets busy on the day they allow you to throw cabbages at Donald Spunk Trumpet.

We bumped our way over to do our first Fast Pass, Splash Mountain in Frontierland, and when we came out, grabbed a pineapple Dole Whip and had a grown-up discussion about how long we wanted to stay here.

The arguments were concise and sounded like this.

For the defence - we'd paid a fortune to be here, we knew it was gonna be busy and we might never come here again.

For the prosecution - it's too busy, we can't actually DO anything and it's not an enjoyable experience.

In the end, we agreed wholeheartedly that despite the crowds we should stick it out so decided to stay until at least Mr Disney set the fireworks off.

BUT... I'm going to have a rant about this and I'm sure I'm not alone here. It strikes me that old Mr Disney is getting a bit too greedy by allowing so many people in and at the same time may have strayed from the point of making the Magic Kingdom the epicentre of the most Magical Place on Earth by allowing so many of earth's inhabitants to come and share the same few hot square miles of tarmac.

I can find a little bit of misery in everything (I'm from Dudley, that's my job) but despite that even I get soppy and emotional the first time you walk down Moan Street and see the big plastic castle. It's precisely at that moment when you're with your loved ones and look up and see it in the distance, surrounded by the smells from the bakery and the emotional tunes in the background that you realise the financial sacrifices were worth it, and that every penny you've spent getting your tribe over here is fully justified when you see their faces light up and the emotion in their eyes.

But it was different today. Maybe it's cos the kids weren't with us, or we got here at a particularly busy time, but todays experience was definitely lacking that bit of Tinkerbelle dust. The whole place was rammed with folks - absolutely heaving from the entrance by the train station up to the castle and beyond. Every "land" was packed too, and you couldn't walk in a straight line for more than a few yards without some twat bashing into you or having your heels clipped by one of them massive kids' buggies-cum-caravans.

You know it must be bad when you start craving the open, boring spaces of Epcot.

I get that it's gonna be busy, I get that it's probably the worlds most visited tourist attraction (after The Black Country Museum when the scratchings factory has an open day) but surely it makes no sense to allow it to become so unenjoyable that it puts people off from going.

Rant done.

We did what we could by using up our remaining Fast Passes – one for Buzz Lightyear's daft shooting game and the other for the Jungle Cruise (yeah, we Fast Passed that... that's how busy it was) and rounded off the evening with a fabulous but incredibly calorific Disney Dingo Dollar Credits meal somewhere in Adventureland.

This left us with just 452 credits each to use up in the next three days... how on earth are you supposed to eat this much food?? I reckon Mr Disney should definitely give you some sort of prize for completing the course, like a 6 week trial of the Cambridge Diet or a voucher for Jacamo.

With a food baby in my belly and a big hole in my wallet, we wobbled over to a packed Main Street to try and find a spot where we could catch the tiniest glimpse of the fireworks / lightshow. And we did – we managed to find a three-inch gap between a very tall man with a child on his shoulders and a lamppost.

We witnessed this extravagant, multi-million dollar firework finale to our park day via what was the equivalent of viewing a film at the Odeon in Dudley through the slot in a post box.

We left before the end to beat the families to the bus stop, and once back at Mr Disney's Convalescant Retreat for Salty Sea Dogs (aka, The Beach Club), we had the now customary gin and tonic nightcap followed by a deep, deep sleep.

P.S. electrical storms and rain in Skibbereen

Mr Walt Disney
The Big Castle
Magic Kingdom Theme Park
Orlando

Ref: Walking Lanes

Dear Mr Disney,

I hope you are well. I decided to write to you again despite you not answering my first letter about the Adult Magic Hours. I'm not angry that you didn't reply - I'm guessing you're dead busy counting your takings or making all them papier mache rocks for Star Wars Land.

Anyway, I've got another idea and money spinner that I'd like you to consider to make my and many others enjoyment of your Psycho Parks that little bit better.

This one is for the directionally challenged people... ya know, those people that don't seem to be able to walk in a straight line, have no clue where they are going and are oblivious to the world around them

WALKING LANES!

Like on the motorway (or Freeway as you Humericans call it) you could draw lines on the ground and categorise them for different people so they only annoy their own kind:

Lane 1 - The Stopping Lane - identified by a sudden and dramatic stop directly in front of you with no explanation and starts back off again as though nothing has happened.

Lane 2 - The Wandering Lane - possessing non-directional legs that have no obvious connection to their brain, this lane to be fitted with them bumpers like they use at the bowling alley.

Lanes 3, 4 & 5, The Big Stroller Lane. Exclusively for those families who think they need to bring the entire contents of their garage on holiday. And their kids. Includes those little turnip picking trucks popular with Latin American families.

Lane 6 - Candy Crushing Lane, for those so addicted to that pointless, mind frazzling game they have to walk and play at the same time.

Lane 7 - The Big Family Lane - the families that all wear matching t shirts and insist on grouping DIAGONALLY across the pavement. Must all walk in single file. And quietly.

Lane 8 - The Fast Lane, reserved exclusively for The Military Mum. The mum on a mission to make sure everyone is having a great time, so long as they stick to her pre-arranged, laminated, colour coded itinerary. Discipline can be fun.

Hope you like my suggestion. Obviously you don't have to thank me in person, Mr Disney. Just add another 50 or so credits to my Disney Dingo Dollar Dining Plan and we'll call it quits.

Yours sincerely

Disgruntled of Dudley

Michael Hadley

A bit more Epcot Day

Sponsored by Alka Seltzer

It's about day fourteen of our US jaunt, and the restless sleep patter combined with the mountains of chemically processed food and drink we're consuming means that we've reached that stage in any Orlando holiday where you start to have weird dreams.

You know that feeling when you can't sleep properly, so you sort of drift in and out of consciousness whilst in the middle of a bizarre dream that's playing in the background, and you sort of know that you're not fully asleep so don't know if they're true or not?

My dreams last night included skipping around a big lake with a woman dressed as a doughnut being followed by the seven dwarves. Then later on having my tongue pulled out with a big pair of pliers by a cast member at the Quick Service meal till and not being able to say "how many credits is that again?" And at some point I was flying above earth, "Superman" style with a Buzz Lightyear type hero who looked a bit like Terry Wogan.

I know Missus H had a bad dream too. I also know I played a starring role in to too.

Wanna know how I know?

Cos when I woke up she was hovering two inches above my dopey face, staring at me with her angry, menacing eyes and a quivering lip. Before I could utter a word, she screamed:

"You absolute bastard..!"

... and then didn't talk to me for two hours.

I have no idea what I did to upset her so just added it to the growing list of things that I don't understand about her (and all women). I've added a few more and while I'm feeling brave cos she's in the bath, I'll share them now.

Missus H regularly says things that I think relate to the application of makeup, and in particular at that point when I've been ready to go out at the pre-arranged time and she's still sitting in a dressing gown with her hair wrapped in a skanky towel in the shape of a walnut whip.

Me: "Are you nearly ready? We got to be there in 5 minutes..."

Her: "I'm just putting me face on".

Putting her face on!

It's <u>already</u> on!

What does that even mean??

Does she mean she has multiple faces, and whilst I'm not looking swaps them over depending on the mood she's in? If that's true, then I think she needs a little help as she seems to be stuck with her "I'm fucked off with you" face…

Closely followed in weirdness by:

"Just gotta put some eyes on…"

Some eyes? What, like draw some extra ones on? And why… and where? Why would you need more than the two she's already got and where are the other ones going?

And this is a good one – we'll eventually be in the car on our way out and then she'll suddenly and dramatically jolt and scream "Oh my god!" as though we're just about to be hit by a meteor. When the shock dies down and I haven't steered the car into a bush, I ask her "Christ, what is it?"

"I think I left me curlers on".

These curlers are her pride and joy – it's one of them new style ones that's as big as a baguette, get lethally hot in seconds and are so dangerous you have to wear a black, flame-retardant glove to use them.

The same woman that can't remember if she left her curlers on 5 minutes ago is the same woman that can recite the place, time, date, atmospheric temperature, who our MP was and what we were both wearing on each and every occasion I fucked up since we met. And what feeble excuse

160

I'd used in my defence <u>and</u> how long it took for her to forgive me.

She's out of the bath now. I'll have to carry on quick cos she hovers over my shoulder while I'm writing looking for mentions...I might not tell her I published this book at all.

We had a lazyish start to the day today, and not just because she didn't talk to me for what I did in her dream. We were planning on going to The Magical Kingdom again early doors, but after seeing how busy it was yesterday we decided to give it a miss. And also because Guest Services put the phone down on me when I called them to suggest that they stop kids coming in between 12 and 2 to give me chance to ride the Dwarves.

Instead, for the second day running we decided to doss around by the pool for a bit. Now, I'm not a fidgety kind of person by any means but I do find lying around in the sunshine a bit boring unless there's something interesting to look at or I can quickly fall into a power snooze.

I just don't get the sunbathing thing – it's too hot to just lie there being cooked to like a spit-roasted chicken, you can't read a book cos you're having to squint into the sun and suntan cream gets under your eyelids. I'd listen to music but this always end up with me garrotting myself with the headphones lead or getting one of the buds stuck in me earhole.

Worst of all you have to take most of your clothes off, which I've found is a pre-requisite if you want a suntan. Now, I won't go into a great deal of detail here ladies and gents in case you're eating, but my body is the colour, texture and suppleness of an Aldi skinless sausage but with a higher fat content and therefore not best suited to being exposed in front of families.

With my clothes off, I could easily be cast as "Dead Fat Man Number 3" on one of those morgue trollies in Silent Witness.

In contrast Missus H has a great bod and could sunbathe for hours and hours, lying perfectly still and as stiff as two day toast to make sure she gets the perfect tan. Except on the bits I've missed with the suntan cream, obvs.

Unsurprisingly, I soon get bored of the idea of sunbathing so left Missus H to it and headed back indoors to poke about the Beach Club shop, looking for mischief and food… well we have only had 3,000 calories (each) for breakfast and it was nearly 1 o clock.

I did a recce while Missus H sizzled away and weighed up the options available to us, eventually settling on a wonderful little place by the pool called Beaches & Cream, which is a cheesey American type diner in keeping with the old style Beach Club theme.

Beaches and Cream is perhaps the biggest assault on your taste buds, waistline and cholesterol level in all of the eating establishments in Mr Disney's Psycho Parks and hotels, and it makes no excuses for being at the very top of the food chain in terms of sugar and calories. Almost every dish on the menu comes with either syrup, peanut butter or a side of waffles - including the chips.

At Beaches and Cream you can get a months' worth of calories in just a few bites of a triple-decker burger or a few hefty sucks on a malted shake. It's the only restaurant I've ever been to where they have an emergency defibrillator inside each booth and all the waitresses have a little "First Aider" badge to reassure you that they're qualified in CPR.

The signature dish of Beaches and Cream is a truly incredible creation aimed at the real greedy bastards called "The Kitchen Sink". This amazing fete of calorific delight is a carry-on suitcase sized dessert served in a real aluminium kitchen sink complete with taps. The sink is filled with your choice of 6 types of ice cream, topped with choc chips, fudge brownies, whipped cream, glace cherries and a sprinkle of hundreds and thousands, and it looks like the contents of fat man autopsied stomach if his last meal was a catering sized black forest gateaux.

If you think that's too much and you're worried about missing one of your five a day, you can always substitute one of the lumps of brownie for a peanut butter covered banana.

It costs around twenty dollars, but just for an extra five bucks you can have the "Princess Fiona" upgrade which gets you 2 more ice cream flavours, a whole carrot cake crumbled on top and a free pair of elasticated trousers.

We sat and ate our two burgers and chips at the bar while across from us an American couple on the "large" side slowly devoured a sink EACH. And the waitresses were encouraging em to finish it! The whole restaurant seemed to go dead quiet as they reached further down into the bottom of the sink, as though we were all literally watching a slow motion double cardiac arrest.

They still hadn't finished by the time we left for our afternoon stroll around Epcot, but we did see them later on outside the hotel lobby as one of them was being lifted by iron fairy into the back of a strengthened ambulance having fallen into a diabetic coma. They'll get extra Disney Dingo Dollar Dining credits for that, I'll bet.

Before I move on to Epcot, just time for another moan. Who was the cockwomble that came up with the idea to use porous cardboard straws for thick, gloopy milkshakes? The cardboard collapses within a few moments of being in your milkshake leaving you to defy physics by trying to suck a thick, iced liquid up a soggy 5mm cardboard pipe.

Utterly useless...I'm all for saving the planet but come on, surely we can design better straws lads?

Unsurprisingly, I have an idea – as it's all about the turtles not being killed by plastic, why not make the straws with a back scratching attachment so they can get to them dead itchy bits inside the shell? I remember having a plaster cast on my arm when I was a kid and it used to itch like hell, so can you imagine how a turtle must feel? I bet they'd love that AND Mr Disney could add a few bob to the price. Genius or what? I should be an inventor.

Talking of turtles, after the meal I needed to visit the Little Cowboys room and after I'd made way for this evenings meal, we wobbled back to the room to get ready for a few more hours in boring Epcot.

This time we were off to do some of my favourite things, which are all located in the bit that's called "The Sea", namely the Nemo ride, looking at the fish in the aquarium and, continuing the turtle theme, the awesome Turtle Talk with Crush.

I do realise that sentence has made me sound like a nine-year-old.

Nevertheless, I love it over there and with Missus H firmly holding my hand and a giddy skip we headed in through the back gates of the park and made our way over.

On the way, we went past the site of the what was the old Michael Jackson's Captain EO ride / film / crack dream which closed down a few years ago when Mr Disney finally realised that Mickey J was a full on nonce.

Strangely, it has now been replaced by a kiddie's playground. Who said Americans don't do irony?

We bimbled about The Sea for a little while before heading over to Soarin, another one of my fave rides. If you're not familiar with the ride, here's a bit of an insight – after an hour of waiting, you and your fellow Soarers get strapped into a big garden seat and then gently lifted up in the air, directly in front of a massive screen projecting images of iconic areas of the world. The premise is that you "Soar" over said icons so you can get a bird's eye view of what's going on. In a few minutes, you fly from the North Pole to the Sahara Desert stopping off at the Taj Mahal, The Eiffel Tower and a weird looking German castle, before seeing fireworks blasting out over the big Epcot golf ball.

Couple of tips for ya; if, like me, you were expecting to soar over iconic areas of the Black Country like Noddy Holders house or the Wolves ground, be prepared to be disappointed. Also, if at all possible, get yerself seated in one of the middle big garden hammock swingy things – the big screen is slightly on the skunt and if you're on the end it looks like you've just developed walleye.

The first time we did Soarin a few years ago, we sat on the end and I was more than a little concerned about the state of the Eiffel Tower – it looked like it was trying to be pulled out of the ground with some gigantic magnet and was as bent as an EU regulation banana.

I was so worried that I called in at the Embassy inside the French bit of Epcot straight after to report it, but it had closed for the day. Well, it was quarter to ten in the morning, and they'd been at work for a whole 45 minutes.

As previously mentioned, nearly three decades of putting up with me and raising two kids has taken it's toll on Missus H's brain, to the point where she gets her worms muddled up, struggles to finish a sentence and sometime forgets names. Hence why so far on this Disney jaunt, she's asked me when we are going on "Big Munter Mountain" and that after reading great reviews she'd really love to do "An Enchanted Evening with Bev".

Today's corker was inside "The Land" area of Epcot, and a short, informative but very dull ride called "Living with The Land".

This demonstrates how, amongst many other boring things, they are making water cress out of grass cuttings and reclaimed water. For some reason, Missus H really wanted to go on this but couldn't remember the name – hence from now on it will be known as "The Cucumber Ride".

We had fast passes for the new Frozen ride inside Norway, so headed over there next. Just at the start of the Norway bit, there's a dead posh shop selling <u>very</u> expensive Norwegian based tat like whale steaks, pickled herrings and rubberised, seagoing Helly Hansen Sou'westers – perfect when it's 100 degrees outside.

Inside the shop there was a really nice, floral fragrance which I'd immediately taken for Norwegian air freshener. It was, in fact, a dead expensive parfum that they were flogging so it was being pumped out into the shop by a girl over by the harpoon rack.

Missus H really liked this smell so I wondered over to see how much it was gonna cost me.

As I looked over the options (big bottle, small bottle, travel size with extra roll on deodorant and colonic irrigation kit) a young poppet of a cast member called Cherelle Oklahoma (Jacksonville, FL), wandered over and asked me:

"Would you like to smell my Laila?"

Before I could say "I'd love to, bab. Get yer coat" Missus H magically appeared by my side and 30 seconds later I was at the till, handing over 70 bucks for barely an eyeful of a stinky liquid called Laila that smells like Baltic Bog Cleaner.

But... BONUS! The main man, Geir Ness himself was there and he was signing all the bottles!

You know? Geir Ness... the world-famous Norwegian perfume, clothes designer and Thunderbirds puppet lookalike?

No? Me either... (worth a Google. It helps with this next bit)

I don't meet many perfume and clothes designers in the Black Country so I'm not sure if they are all arrogant, botoxed, egotistical pricks or if it was just him. He was obviously sick of being full of himself in Norway so decided to be full of himself in pretend Norway in Epcot, poncing about the place in his tight designer jeans and bleached blonde hair.

I'm not saying he's had a lot of botox, but when he smiled I could see his ball bag twitch.

Anyway, the Norwegian diva managed to grace our presence by making small talk and very kindly sign Missus H's perfume bottle whilst staring at her boobs. He also slipped in a free sample of the men's fragrance for me after I'd asked after his brother, Loch.

After the Frozen ride, we headed slowly out of the park before it got too packed as people were already starting to pick spots to watch the fireworks. We left them to it and instead used up some more Disney Dingo Dollar credits on another all you can scoff meal in the ESPN bar where I had a burger so big I had to dislocate my jaw to eat it, before a slow, drunken meander back to Mr Disney's Retirement Home For Ex Seamen (aka The Beach Club).

We were both exhausted by this point in the holiday – only a few days in but already the heat, jet lag and food had left us totally knackered.

So with weird thoughts of cucumbers, botoxed Norwegians and Michael Jackson dressed as an alien, we fell fast asleep, ready for more fun tomorrow at the Animal Kingdom.

P.S. She forgot to check the weather in Skibbereen. Assume it was raining.

The 14 hour Animal Kingdom Day

This exciting chapter is proudly bought to you by our new sponsor, Holly Willoughby's Bone Balm, the new treatment to ease early morning stiffness.

We've reached the stage on this eating and marching holiday where I have no idea what day it is (I'm guessing it's somewhere between day 8 and 10), all acts of personal hygiene have gone out of the window and every bone in my body is aching from the daily 25,000 steps recorded happily on Missus H's FitBit.

I'm so stiff that when I get up in the morning I've taken on the walking mannerism of C3PO, shuffling around with little steps looking like I'm trying to carry something with clenched buttocks whilst my arms are outsplayed to keep my balance and prevent me from bumping in to the walls.

It's obviously had a continued effect on Missus H's brain too. As previously mentioned, she does get her words muddled up and the heat, the lack of sleep, the over eating and strenuous exercise has taken further toll on her ability to speak actual words. Hence today she had three stabs at Flight of Passage:

"Are we doing Flighty Passage today? What is it again...? Avatars Passing? Pandoras Passage?"

"I got it! Flight of The Avatar?"

Nearly right. We all know it's called Flight of Sausage.

So at 07.30 with hangovers from last night's gin, we boarded one of Mr Disney's trump powered buses bound for the Animal Kingdom.

I love Flight of Sausage. It's still the best ride in any of the Orlando parks by some distance, and well worth the 2 hour, hot, bad tempered queue we experienced this morning with raging hangovers, no water and no shade.

Queues are good for material though...

What's with the calf tattoos folks? I don't get it at all, especially on women. Now, I'm not against tattoos (I have 2, thanks for asking and no you can't see em) but this is a new phenomenon to me and something to add to the loooong list of things that baffle me about women. I'd put calf tattoos as a new entry, straight in at number 3, behind the mood changes at 2.

Nothing will dislodge number 1 - having the heating on before the August bank holiday and still walking around in layers upon layers of "comfies"... and STILL feeling cold.

Anyway, calf tattoos. One young lady in front of me had yellow angel wings on a bed of thorns, that from a distancc looked like a hi viz jacket surrounded by tangled fishing line.

I spotted another older lady who had a purple flowering vine wrapped around calf which actually looked quite nice... until I got closer and realised they were varicose veins.

Flight of Sausage completed and as thrilled as we were the first time we did it (awesome, awesome, awesome ride – one of the best ever) we headed back to Animal Kingdom and a short trek to Africa

After a poachers breakfast of rhino bacon and scrambled dodo egg, we boarded a bus pretending to be driven by a failed actor for a look at some bored homesick animals. I can't remember what it was called - my guess is Didier Drogbas Safari Lurch Lorry.

You would think given all his money, Mr Disney can afford to fill in some of them potholes, or at least get some lorries with better suspension.

Luckily the Lurch Lorry came to a stop just before the reappearance of my scrambled dodo eggs, and we headed off for a tour around the park.

We managed to do Yeti (twice), It's Tough To Be A Bugs Life, Dinosaur, Finding Nemo, The Musical (which is utterly, utterly fantastic) before meeting up with a delightful girl called Lucy Wragg. Eagle eyed Disney nerds may remember Lucy from her "single mummy blog" back in 2017 – indirectly she is the reason I started blogging, so it's all her fault.

After a scrummy late afternoon lunch / early dinner using FOUR Dingo Dollar Dining Plan Credits (you know it's posh when the writing on the menu is small) we headed back to the Flighty Passage area to check out the wait time and use our last fast pass on the Na'vi River Journey. This is a gentle river rapids type ride that floats you gently through bioluminescent set pieces typical of the planet Pandora, home to the Na'vi people. It has the most modern and complex audio animatronics and was heralded as a Disney masterpiece in it's portrait of the film and potential life on another planet.

Shit compared to It's A Small World.

However, it did spark another one of my inner thoughts. I do find Avatar women weirdly attractive.

I just said that out loud, didn't I?

The slim legs, the tall athletic build and long arms. Nothing pervy, it's just be easier for them to adjust the TV aerial.

Bizarrely, the crowds had disappeared so we managed to get on Flight Of Sausage one last time before heading back to Mr Disney's Rest Home For Destitute Marines (aka The Beach

Club) for our last night's sleep in a Disney property.

Moving Day

Sponsored by Pickfords.

So today was our last day with Mr Disney before heading over to spend a bit of time with his evil cousin and nemesis, Mr Universal.

We were in no rush so asked for a late check out and packed up whilst watching American TV – more specifically, the adverts.

I love American TV adverts, me.

The sheer, shameless audacity and barefaced lying of American advertisers is amazing. The ad execs obviously believe that the TV watching public is totally dumb, which gives them free license to hoodwink the audience into believing any old shite as long as there's a catchy jingle or the product / service is being sold by a hot soccer mum or handsome jock.

I've watched a lot of these on my trips to the US, and I reckon since Donald Spunk Trumpet incredibly became president it got worse. Or funnier, whichever way you take it.

Maybe the American public has got so used to the bullshit coming from the White House that they've become immune to it all – the nations bullshit filter has been eroded to such a degree that advertisers wholeheartedly believe that they can use any lies to push their products into the homes of a lie-weary nation.

176

You believe Trump's not a racist? Great! Buy some unicorn eggs! Each one a double-yoker!

Don't think that Trump sexually assaulted all those women? Awesome!! How would you like to invest in my cousin's Nigerian bank?

You agree that it isn't true when people call Trump a roaring racist, homophobic, misogynist, narcissistic orange faced oaf? Wow! Have I got just the thing for you – Magic Beans! Just plant 6 and your beanstalk will grow all the way to Russia!

The absolute best TV ads are the ones for medicines that claim to fix whatever your ailment is, *whilst telling you that it may cause the ailment you already have*!

How clever is that? Utter genius!

Every medicine advert is about 2 minutes long. The first 30 seconds are set at a dreamy pace, shot through a filtered lens and tells you how this medicine is gonna change your life for the better. It's going to cure all your ailments, make you a better, happier person and increase your cock length by 10%. All this accompanied by footage of a healthy-looking individual throwing a football to his beautiful kids or wearing an apron whilst cooking at a smoky barbecue with his family and the pet Labrador.

Then the plot twist.

The next 90 seconds is shot through a darker lens accompanied by a fast scrolling list of all the ailments this medicine can cause. All narrated by a different bloke altogether: one who's just had a big suck of helium and proceeds to tell you that it's highly likely that this drug has such severe side effects that it's almost certain to cause not only your own horrific, painful agonising death but your family, everyone at the barbecue, everyone you've ever met and anyone you're ever likely to meet in the future before you die.

Even the Labrador.

The fascination with drugs (as in the good type that fix you, not the bad type that make you happy) is not just confined to the crazy world of TV advertising though. It's massive business in America, in stark contrast to what we're used to in the UK, because there is a lot of money to be made by the big corporations. Hence the reason why the politicians don't want free healthcare in the States – there's a lot of people getting very, VERY rich off the back of people being ill.

(It's the same with guns – it's a multi-billion industry in the US and controlled largely by the National Rifle Association. No Republican politician who craves power will stand up to the NRA and campaign for tighter gun laws as they know that when it comes to donations, which completely fund their election campaigns, a big chunk of the money comes from the NRA and its supporters. So what if a few thousand get killed each year cos some dumb fuck watched too many snuff movies and bought a gun from Walmart? A few kids, gays or Muslims getting mown down is a tiny price to pay for the greedy guys at the top making all the money who still believe in a part of the Constitution that was only written 250 years ago).

To back up how crazy the medical / pharmacy industry is over here, and how desperate they are to make it easy for lazy hypochondriacs to get terribly expensive but convenient remedies, over here they have "Drive Thru" pharmacies.

Drive Thru pharmacies!!

How lazy must you be that you can't be bothered to get out of your car to go and buy some paracetamol? No wonder they're all unwell.

And they're not just to collect prescriptions. You can drive up to a window and order pretty much anything you want without having to get out of your car. If you don't have the physical energy to get out of a car, walk 30 yards to the store and get your own Veet, then I'm afraid there's no hope for you.

The Drive Thru concept does fascinates me though and I wonder if we are clever enough for it to catch on in the Black Country...

Imagine this at a Boots the Chemist Drive Thru in deepest West Bromwich, where Mia-Keegen has been struck down with that common ailment that seems to affect a lot of chavvy ladies – a water infection. She pulls up in her pink Citroen Saxo:

(You need to channel your inner Noddy Holder now. You've all got one)

Bab at the window: "Allo, mar name is Destinaaaay. Con ar tek yower orda purleese?"

Mia-Keegen: "Oroight bab, Con aer get wun extra-large tub of Ladybitzbalm with a side o natrel yogut?"

Bab: "Ar'm afrayed we ay got bo natrel yogut. The yogut machine's just bost"

Mia-Keegen: "Fuck. Ok, ar'll ave the strawberry and peach instead"

Bab: "Oroight. Dun yow wanna Go Large for an extra pahnd? Yow con have a bottle of cranberry juice and a tube of Cystablastine"

Mia-Keegen: "Ar gew on then. Oh, an throw in a family bukit of Tena Lady wud ya bab? Ar'm reading that buk by Mykul Hadley"

Bab: "He's a funny chap ay he? That's fourteeeen pahnd fifteee purleeese. Droive rahnd to the next windo when yow con"

Anyroad, back to the story and we squeezed a few lazy hours at the pool. Missus H sunbathed while I went through the Disney Dingo Dollar

Dining Plan invoice to see what we'd used (in other words, have I had my money's worth). It turns out, we had. I could tell this not by calculating the cost of each item but by virtue of the fact that this morning I had to reach for my Marks and Spencer Action Shorts with the elasticated waist.

When I slip these baby's on, I know it's been money well spent.

Turns out I'd got 2 snack credits left, which I used on a breakfast muffin and a yoghurt. I had asked to trade them for a half bottle of Donald Duck gin, but Marie-lou Layleeeen Arizona behind the til said no.

Showered and ready to check out, I shouted to Missus H to see if she was done. In true womanly fashion, she'd chosen this precise moment to start to fill in her HMRC Self-Assessment, as well as retuning the tv, fixing a broken drawer and mending the mini bar.

I've learnt not to argue so busied myself making sure I'd nicked all the Disney shampoos, conditioners, vanity kits and soap to save buying my mum a present (she'll think they're genuine. Sssshhh... don't tell her...).

Around 45 minutes after we were supposed to check out, Missus H shouts "Come on dickhead, I'm waiting for you" and we head out the door and down to reception.

After I've said goodbye to the room. I always do that. Always.

We handed our 7 (Yes, SEVEN) bags to the guy on baggage, Hunter Jaxxon Le Bronx Jr, and headed off to Disney Springs for a late lunch.

Due to the combination of spare cash, no backbone and the enormous measures that American barmen pour, I can't remember much after that.

All I do remember is being on a dockside bar on my own while Missus H went tat shopping. Also, it was hot, I was thirsty, and the little devil inside me thought it would be a fun game to try all the cocktails on the menu. Like a kid in a sweet shop with a months' worth of pocket money and no parental guidance, the little devil won and I got absolutely, well and truly, completely and utterly, spectacularly pissed.

Missus H returned later to find me slumped up a corner wearing a pair of child's Disney ears I'd found hanging off a pram, singing "It's A Small World" surrounded by empty cocktail glasses. Surprisingly, she didn't throw me in the lake but instead joined me in a few cocktails. Her little devil must have won too.

With stonking headaches and several hundred dollars worse off cos of the cocktails and Missus H buying Molly the Cockapoo a bag full of

Disney toys, we headed back to The Beach Club to collect our gear and move out.

We were heading for the dark side for the rest of our holiday... Universal Studios.

P.S. Pissed down all day in Skib.

Hello Universal!

Bought to you by our new sponsor, Werthers Originals for men who just like to be left alone for a bit of peace and quiet.

Our destination for the last few nights of this holiday / endurance test is Portofino Bay, an Italian themed hotel built around a pretend fishing bay based on an actual village in Italy.

The attention to detail is incredible. Not only do they have beautiful terracotta buildings, fake lambrettas and fancy pizza parlours but also swarthy waiters who were talking with their hands and eyeing up Missus H's bosoms. In true Italian fashion, one of them pinched her bum and then ran off when I offered to fight him.

So the second day of our Universal adventure started pretty much the same as the first - stiff, knackered and in need of a power nap within 10 minutes awake.

I'm of a certain age now where I pick and choose which bits of information are important to me, which can, in certain circumstances, lead to a lot of trouble. Today, like most days in my life, was no exception and led to the only disagreement Missus H and I had all holiday.

Which park is the Harry Potter bit in.

Before all you muggles shout out, I know it's in

BOTH parks. But, my dilemma is that I've got to get the right answer in my head before I say it. This isn't necessarily the right answer, just the one that Missus H *thinks* is right.

So we end up playing a game where I'm looking for clues and hints in her early morning mumblings, not helped by the fact that she's completed TikTok, used a Snapchat filter to make me look like a cabbage and spent 20 minutes face timing the dog. No wonder her brains frazzled.

In no chronological order, these are a short collection of the womanly mumblings from which I have to guess what we're doing today.

"We're doing Harry Potter today aren't we? Good cos I want to go on Star Tours. Then cos we're close by, can we do the Hypocrit Ride and get some of that Buttock Beer?" Then walk to The Hulk and stop off for lunch at Bubba Humps? Then I just want to pop back to Disney Springs cos I need a Mickey Waffle for my sister's dog".

A blind mouse in an escape room would have a better sense of direction.

I can't confess to being much better. I know both parks as "Universal" and if we need to go somewhere it's either "the park on the right with that big ball" or "the park on the left by the crashed seaplane".

After a long splash n snooze in the hotel pool, we caught the pretty little ferry boat that connects the posh, outer hotels to Universal itself and decided to start in "the park on the right with that big ball". This led us through the wacky Dr Seuss section, past the weird non-discernible Middle Eastern bit with the rides no-one ever goes on, and then on to Harry Potter Land.

I've mentioned before that unlike Missus H who is a right mug(gle) I don't "get" the Harry Potter thing.

Not cos I don't like the films but cos I went to school with a kid called Harry Potter and every time I hear his name, I get flashbacks to being bullied at Dudley Comprehensive.

It left me scarred, just like Harry's brow.
I was quite a weedy little kid, and I looked like a girl (hard to imagine now I'm such a butch stud muffin) so I was always getting my head flushed down the bog or having my lunch money nicked. I had so many wedges my mum thought I was wearing a G string to school.

I was quite looking forward to spending time in Potter Land as I wanted to check out the new ride that everyone had been queuing 10 hours for called, rather catchily, Hagrid's Magical Creatures Motorbike Adventure.

Strangely enough, it's not the first time I've ridden a big unit called Hagrid, but I'd rather not go into that right now. Suffice to say that this was a much enjoyable, and far less painful, experience. No spoilers, but it's great.

We spent a good few hours ambling around the top bit of Harry Potter Land, drinking butter beer (that's just expensive ice cream soda isn't it?) before we caught the train which transports you to the other bit - ya know, the bit with Gringotts, the fire breathing dragon and the wobbly shops.

We agreed to split up for a while so Missus H could spend 30 minutes in each and every shop.

Wonky Emporium Ecspensivo!

While Missus H had a poke around looking for cheap tat to buy as souvenirs for all the hundreds of nieces and nephews I neither know or like, I amused myself by laughing at the failed attempts of hundreds of kids who are melting in long, black cloaks trying to make a frog "ribbet" in a shop window or make a book twitch 3 inches on a shelf by wafting an $95 thin plastic wand at it.

Parento Gulleebalis!

Aren't these kids roasting? I'm literally melting like Olaf on a sunbed, my pants are wringing wet and the soles of my Aldi trainers are peeling off with each hot step, yet there's kids in thick BLACK full length cloaks! Bet that was an interesting conversation getting ready this morning.

Temper tantrum infantium!

Missus H reappeared briefly to hand me loads of bags full of expensive tat before announcing excitedly that she was off to find hoops, a quaffle, three bludgers, and an extra thick broomstick. For a split second I thought she'd rediscovered her sadomasochistic side until I realised she meant all the gear needed to play Quidditch.

That was a mighty relief to me as I didn't fancy dressing up as a baby again and I'd forgotten our safe word.

I've just read that playing Quidditch is an actual thing now and there are teams and leagues for it in America. (Yeah, had to be America didn't it?). If you get a minute after this chapter, just Google "Is Quidditch a real sport" and see for yourself.

I can see the attraction of sticking something in your hoop (I was young and adventurous once) but for the absolute life of me I don't get why they run around with a broom stick between their legs pretending to fly. But then you realise that these are Americans – the same country that bought us Tiger King, Donald Spunk Trumpet and Weird Al Yankovic and who think that grits are real food.

Yankee Imbecilicus!

She wandered off so I continued my poke about the wobbly shops looking for both writing material and aircon.

I found both.

I'm thinking of writing a Black Country version of Harry Potter, based on my old school mate of the same name but set in Dudley. Like Diagonal Alley, Dudley has a lot of dark, dingy shops selling tat, they're all on the skunt cos of the old mine shafts and the streets are full of witches, goblins and weirdos.

Especially outside Wetherspoons.

The school isn't a problem – gonna call that Bogwarts. We've got loads of battered old comprehensives to use as boarding schools where the kids will be fed a daily diet of scratchings, faggots and peas and "concrete cake" (Black Country fruit loaf), washed down with pints of Banks's Mild.

I've already decided that in the film version Noddy Holder will be headmaster, Lenny Henry the caretaker and Julie Walters will play the nit nurse.

The kids will be sorted into houses by putting on Noddy's Top Hat. The houses are called:

> ➢ Slippitin
> ➢ Grippingball

> ➢ Cameltow and
> ➢ Musclepuff

Each kid will be taught real wizardry like how to magically remove a catalytic converter, how to dodge a car park fine and how to find Michael McIntyre funny.

Every so often over the faggot and pea supper, Noddy will yell "IT'S CHRIIIISSSTMAAAASSSS!!!" and one lucky wizard will be given a season ticket on the halfway line at Wolverhampton Wanderers.

Instead of Quidditch, the clever little wizards will play British Bulldog with pick axe handles replacing broom stales with points awarded if you don't spill blood or break a collar bone.

I got really excited about this idea and I really reckoned I was on to something. I went into the nearest shop, Quality Quidditch Supplies and spoke to a nice young lad called Dick Hunter behind the till.

Dick was dressed in his full Hufflepuff Hoop Beater gear and we had a lovely chat. He listened intently to my idea and then I asked if he had JK Rowley's phone number. Turned out he hasn't but he did give me his own, which was nice.

Fantastico Bumboy!

Missus H caught up with me just as Dick was just

about to show me his hoop and we scurried away for our evening's entertainment.

We ate at one of my all-time favourite places, Bubba Gumps, then headed off to Margaritaville for some fab country music washed down with mind blowing cocktails.

And so to bed.

P.S.- plague of locusts in Skibbereen with a 90% chance of rain

Hello SeaWorld!

Sponsored by Captain Findus

We had a bit of a lie in this morning (we got up at 07.00 instead of 06.30 – wowzer) which meant that Missus H had a little longer than usual to go through her morning routine.

This is a new routine that she's had a FitBit for her birthday and means that she now can't wait to wake up so she can check how long she's been asleep for.

Someone make sense of that one (1)

It was quite interesting for the first 20 seconds the first time she did it this holiday, and I feigned extra interest in the hope that as she was now wide awake, I'd either get a cup of tea or some early morning nuptials.

I got neither.

So now I have to lie there and in between disinterested snoozes I get a little nudge and the bright screen of the watch shoved in my dozy face...

"Oooh look, I was awake 5 times in the night... that's you snoring that is..."

(10 second pause while she swipes and digests the next bit of sleep data)

"I've only had 1 hour 22 minutes of deep sleep…"

(Swipe and pause)

"Mind you, 22% of my sleep was REM, which is good…"

(Swipe and long pause)

"I don't like that Michael Stipes"

(Even longer pause)

"Ooh look! It's raining all day In Skibbereen. Have you made me a cup of coffee yet?"

After another battle to make any sort of palatable hot drink with an American coffee machine that was the size of a Toyota Yaris, we propped ourselves up in bed and did what most married couples do when they get time alone. She Candy Crushed or played Solitaire and I checked Twitter to see if Donald Spunk Trumpet had set fire to Mexico yet.

We could afford a bit of a lie in this morning cos we weren't gonna be as mad busy today – we were going to Seaworld and from previous experience the fish don't wake up til lunchtime.

I really like Seaworld - I know it's not everyone's cup of clam chowder and for many falls into the same category as zoos and safari parks in terms of keeping animals in captivity. I'm firmly on the fence on this one – all I can say is from my experience, Seaworld seem to do a hell of a lot to promote marine conservation and raise awareness of sea pollution so I'm happy to fork out my hard-earned bucks for a day's fishy entertainment.

And because they make fab fish tacos.

One other reason that I like Seaworld cos it's quite a small park, you can generally walk places without bumping into stupid people and you don't have to queue ages for the rides. Today was just like that and as soon as we arrived, we were way more relaxed than any day when we'd been to anyone of the Disney Psycho Parks or Universal.

It's also a very pretty park, with lots of open spaces beautifully framed by well-maintained gardens and big, wide flowerbeds. I like it a lot.

As it's generally quiet, there was no mad rush for us to do anything on arrival so Missus H had the customary "pop to the loo".

Which brings me neatly on to #3564 in the things that baffle me about women – the number of times she needs the loo.

It's the first thing we have to do in the parks – locate all the nearest conveniences so that at any point where she feels the need, she doesn't have to mince very far for ablutions. It sometimes happens in an instant – one second she's by my side, then she'll suddenly stop and abruptly disappear like an Olympic walker, shouting over her shoulder "I'm going to squeeze a wee…".

She sometimes goes even when she doesn't need to go "just in case…"

To be fair I think she was having a tough M day today. It started with the frustration of not being able to Facetime Molly the Cockapoo (I think Molly had her phone on plane mode) and continued with not being able to choose which pair of 10 identical brown strappy wedges she wanted to wear. In the end she opted for her new Bobble Soul trainers, even though she said "trainers with nobbly bottoms make my bum go all funny…"

Someone make sense of that one (2)

Like most Grumpy blokes, I've learned not to question and go along with it.

Anyway, back in the park and the first thing we do is sit in the beautiful late morning sunshine with a nice coffee and a pot of jellied eels and make a sort of plan for shows, feeding times, loo breaks etc.

We stopped quite near the entrance and as the morning guests arrive, they're collared for the obligatory $25.00 souvenir photo with Doug The

Dolphin or Wally The Whale or whatever Mr Seaworld is calling these scruffy, threadbare costumed freaks.

We watched with interest as the photographer tried to drum up trade from passing families, most of whom seemed totally ambivalent to having their picture taken with a grown man in a fish suit. That was until a Japanese family walked in and saw Wally The Whale and excitedly ran off to the gift shop to buy a harpoon.

We drained our coffees having made the plan to do all the exciting ride stuff first thing so we could eat our lunch safe in the knowledge that there'd be no chance of chucking up me shark fin soup all over some poor unsuspecting tourist off the top of Kraken.

First up was Manta.

Manta is an interesting experience. For those of you that may not have tried it out, it's the one where you're strapped in sitting down as normal in a row of four across. Then, after a teenage ride operator that I wouldn't trust to tie his own shoe laces but is now in charge of my families inheritance wiggles the harness to make sure you're safe, you are hoisted up and backwards so you're facing the floor.

Dangling, if you like.

On lift off you're then facing forwards on the ride – great if you're at the front but for everyone else you get a full on view of other peoples feet (as mentioned, Missus H is a podiatrist so she loved this bit. "Ooooh, he's got a nasty callus". Freak).

The premise is that in this prone position you can "fly" like a Manta Ray... swooping and diving, soaring and climbing, twisting and rolling at breakneck speed.

It's horrible.

There was no queue at all, so we were on in no time. As I'm a complete and utter scaredy cat, I always close my eyes on the ascent and try to find my happy place to convince myself I'm not on a roller coaster at all.

I have three happy places – fishing on the river Wye, watching Wolves at Molineux and burying my head in Missus H's ample bosoms. Today I chose the fishing one and with lids shut tight it was working... until we went up and over the first climb and I realised that the G Force was so strong I couldn't open my eyes again.

In between screams, trumps and Missus H shouting "open yer eyes ya wimp!" I managed to free my hands and peel them open – only to find that the same G Force now had them permanently and worryingly wide open and my eyeballs were completely exposed.

It was an interesting ride photo – Missus H's expression is perfect and her face is a picture of utter adrenaline fuelled joy, while I look like I've been freeze framed after taking a punch from Mike Tyson and someone has stuck wiggly eyes on me.

After surviving Manta and not feeling such a wimp, we went on to do the two mega coasters - Mako and Kraken. They were both awesome.

Mako is an interesting experience. It looks like it's been made from Meccano and stands on little skinny legs in the middle of a man-made lake (filled with crocodiles, obviously). It's the biggest rise and drop I think I've ever experienced and the only time I've ever felt like I was actually falling – the drop makes you come out of your seat so for a split second you feel totally weightless.

Loved it. So much so we went on it twice.

It was almost time for some fish food and the afternoon shows and we only had one ride left to do – Infinity Falls. This is a river rapids type thingy which boasts the tallest drop of any water ride in the world. It had not been open too long so I was keen to go on – however, Missus H refused to do it, saying "I don't do spladoosh rides" cos it might get her hair wet.

And here's #3565 in the things that baffle me about women.

What's the big deal with women getting their hair wet? Missus H's like that ALL the time. Whether we're in a swimming pool, water park, Aldi... one sign of water and she's off in a panicked:

"Aaarrgggh, don't!! I doh wanna get me hair wet today".

Even on the hottest, sunniest day and I've managed to get her in to a pool she'll try to extend her neck like ET to keep even the straggly neck bits of hair out of the water as she doggy paddles from side to side.

I couldn't persuade her so went solo rider with a lovely family from Mexico and walked off ten minutes later wetter than an otter's bum bag.

We had lunch by one of the pools – I had a sandwich containing some of the brothers and sisters of fish we'd seen in the aquarium and Missus H had a prawn so undercooked I reckon if she'd chucked it back in it'd had a 50 / 50 chance of survival.

After lunch, we rounded off our wonderful day with a few of the shows on offer.

We did the obligatory Killer Whale show and watched on as unsuspecting families at the front got soaked, followed by the Seal Lions debacle which is neither entertaining or interesting and is humiliating for the poor creatures. Oh and it *really* stinks of fish. We sat near the front and I swear one big Seal looked me in the eye and said "save me, mate. This is awful". If I was in charge of Seaworld I'd bin this show and free the Seal Lions to live a happier life back in the ocean or at Gandeys Circus.

We just about made the last Dolphin show before they were all put to bed for the night.

I LOVE the dolphin show. Not just cos they're amazingly intelligent, beautiful creatures but because it reminds me of when I once was part of a little gang of mates that used to meet up and discuss these stunning creatures called the Dudley Dolphin Society.

I was gonna go on to do it as a career, but two things stopped me – there's not much call for dolphin trainers in Dudley and I fell out with me dolphin mates when they started getting a bit clicky.

We swam on til our fins were dropping off and left the park almost as it closed, ready for another big night out at Universal Citywalk.

Sorry to all you parents I have to say that Citywalk without kids is so much more fun... we got plastered (again), we had a great meal (again) and watched some great live music. It was one of the very few moments when we were glad we didn't have kids in tow.

Ended another wonderful day with an overdose of Voodoo Donuts which resulted a few hours later in a scary fever dream about a talking Sea Lion who worked in my factory as a fork lift driver. It was so bad Missus H had to calm me down by holding my head in her bosom.

I'll try that one again.

PS – It actually was raining all day in Skibbereen. Told ya.

Our Last Universal Day

Sponsored by Dr. Phil McAvity and the team at Kissimee Whitening Lightning Dental Clinic.

Welcome back for our last day in Universal Studios. I do apologise for the lack of exact detail in these chapters – as previously stated this book is by no means a guide to any of the parks and if I went into every aspect of each and every single thing we did while we were here, I'd have lost you in the California bit.

I'm happy to leave that level of scrutiny to the hundreds of you lovely bloggers that like to go into minute detail about each moment, describe every step taken (literally) and add 100's of pictures of each day.

Especially of food. Receipts. Calories consumed. Money spent. Places to eat.

Oh, and what little Johnny did today and oh how we laughed... kuh, what's he like eh...?

Good on you all and sorry for being a cynical git, but that's just not for me - as you can probably tell from my ramblings. The only resemblance to reality in my blogs to this point is that I was actually in Orlando. The rest is nonsense.

On to the final few days of our mega vacation and I've come to the conclusion that there is a direct correlation between the length of a holiday and the decline in personal hygiene. We've been away now for over 20 days - since day 14 we hadn't a single of item of clothing that wasn't dirty, by day 16 we'd run out of clean underwear and by day 18, despite bringing 96 kilos of luggage, we've used up the last deodorant.

In an effort to reclaim some dignity, I bought a Goofy hat with flopping ears on a string to cover up my matted hair and Missus H is just wearing a Mumu dress she fashioned from the bedroom curtains.

I decided to give my teeth a proper brushing this morning. I would have been better off with a jet wash and wire wool. By the time I'd finished, I was rinsing out a yellowy brown froth the same colour as mustard.

On a Farrow and Ball chart, it'd be "Earthy Ochre".

Anyway, the nonsense started early today as it's probably our last chance to spend time in the parks, so we headed in to "the park on the left with the crashed seaplane" around 9ish.

I love that first walk into a park, don't you? The sense of excitement and the anticipation of a fun filled day, accompanied by the sights, smells and sounds of a multibillion-dollar theme park ready for another day of till filling entertainment.

Fab.

It hasn't escaped me that some of the rides are now being sponsored by big companies, so Universal can add that extra bit of revenue. For example, the first ride we did today, Hulk, is now sponsored by MaxiMuscle Whey Protein. Spiderman is bought to you by Silly String and Kong, Skull Island is in association with Gorilla Tape.

Over in "the park on the right with the big ball", Men In Black is backed by M Balm & Sons Orlando Funeral Parlour, Rip Ride Rockit is sponsored by Viagra and Transformers is bought to you by The Loppitov Clinic for gender re-assignment.

So, we started on day off with a go on the Hulk rollercoaster, which is absolutely, breathtakingly brilliant and then headed back on ourselves to a quiet little café for some breakfast muffins and coffee. I love finding little quiet, secretive bits that aren't usually busy and this café is one of those-tucked away on the right just at the end of the first walkway, after the sweet shops. Don't tell anyone though, best to keep it secret.

The only thing I could find to moan about here, which is a recurring theme for a café like this, is why can't you just get normal milk? You can get soya, almond, oat, pea (uh?) and creamer that looks like paint but not just normal milk out of a cow.

That creamer stuff is too much for me, so Missus H and I went halves in a half n half, then worked our way up through (ironically) the Marvel bit.

Which Missus H was particularly happy about as it was perfectly timed to see the arrival of Captain America, Spiderman and a few other lycra clad pals with huge bulging crotches. She lapped it up like a giddy schoolgirl and got straight in the queue for the Captain – I don't see the attraction myself. I mean, what has the tall, handsome, charming, muscular, butch guy with strong buttocks so tight that you could crack walnuts in them, got that I haven't?

Pah.

I don't get the obsession with superheroes – not cos I'm against them or anything but because I'm offended that there's never been one with a Black Country accent.

I mean, c'mon… yow've got yer Spidermon, yow've got yer Batmon, yow've got yer Iron Mon… worrabaht Black Country Mon?

Ar con see it nah, he gets his super powas from aytin The Mighty Bag O Scratchins, he flies thru the air with a winged cape in the shape of a kipper tie an' has got jet propelled platform shews. His catchfraaese wud be:

"Black Country Mon ta tha reskew – ar'm gunna saeve ya bab!"

I might write to Mr Universal about this.

He owes me a favour after my last stay here when he really, REALLY offended me by overlooking Barry Manilow in the Hard Rock Hall of Fame, so I hope he'll take heed this time. And because he'll have an excuse to build another big 3D ride to replace that god awful "Toon Town" area that looks like it's trapped in the 60's.

Maybe it's because I have no connection with any of these American characters such as Betty Boo, Popeye or Hagar the Horrible. My growing up coincided with the golden age of kids TV in the 70's and early 80's, so we were treated to normal kids' stuff Rainbow, Button Moon and Tiswas.

Now you're talking.

If you're reading, Mr Universal, get something built as an homage to Zippy and Bungle or a fit bird in fishnets as Sally James and this area would be packed to the rafters every day. Imagine the fun kids would have as the Phantom Flan Flinger turned up, or they got spat on by Bob Carolgees dog!

Don't go overboard with the 70's stuff mind. I'd skip the "Paint By Numbers" classes with Rolf Harris. And definitely, definitely, don't open that craft shop called "Jim'll Fix It"

Honestly though, this whole area needs a makeover as it does look really dated. Weird, odd, shaped characters, funny looking shops selling tat nobody wants, people hanging around looking gormless in a daze cos they can't comprehend what's in front of them.

A bit like being in Walsall High Street.

We carried on a bit further up the road and I very nearly persuaded Missus H to accompany me on Dudley Do Right's Ripsaw Falls, promising that I'd treat her to that special looking truncheon shaped thing she'd seen with a picture of Captain America on it. We stood and watched as folks screamed and got soaked, prompting her to mince off telling me she's not going on it as she doesn't want "a day's worth of soggy crotch irritation…".

Fair play. I wasn't that bothered about Dudley Do Right's anyway as the last time I went on it I'd just washed my pants in the hotel shower and obviously didn't rinse the soap out properly, leading to me walking with a frothing ball bag.

On we marched and went on the excellent "Kong", which had been called everything but by Missus H, including Skong, King Kong Land and The Big Monkey Ride. I love this ride, it's ace.

Even though it was our last Universal Day and God knows when we'd be back again, we were both knackered. We'd had a full on few weeks and probably all parked out. The final straw was when we saw the huge queue for the Jurassic Park thing, so we decided to bale - the luxury of the hotel pool and a booze fuelled afternoon nana nap was calling.

On the way out, we managed to get an Iron Man deodorant and matching Dr Seuss "Thing 1, Thing 2" underpants so we could be clean and ready for our big date night later – The Blue Man Group!

After a wonderful few hours by the pretend Italian Spa hotel pool, listening to pretend Italian Dean Martin and drinking pretend Aperol Spritz cocktails, we douched ourselves down, chucked on the least smelly clothes we had left and caught the ferry boat back to the epicentre of Universal fun.

The Blue Man Group is a Universal icon. We hadn't been before as we couldn't persuade the kids to do anything but coasters, so this was a first for us and we were really excited.

Like us, if you've never been because it doesn't nibble your cheese, please go.

It's funny, bonkers, hilarious, mad, and totally unlike anything I've ever seen before. And I've seen West Bromwich Albion play.

Even me with my bizarre sense of humour and ability to exaggerate couldn't dream of inventing such a weird show – three big, butch blokes with totally blue faces and wide, gawpy eyes, drumming with paint.

Throughout the show, they find new ways to amaze and astonish - spitting out food, abusing the audience, performing mad stunts and getting loads and loads of laughs.

All by just looking at each other and without saying a single word. Not a peep.

It's hilarious.

Go. You won't regret it.

And so to bed after a few cheeky Martinis in the hotel bar and a singalong with a balding Italian crooner tribute act called Perry Comover.

Back tomorrow for my last day in paradise.

P.S.- cloudy with a chance of meatballs in Skibbereen.

Discovery Cove and Hooters (and my birthday)

Sponsored by Victor's Secret, the number one choice for sensual chubby men.

The Victor's Secret idea came to me today when we were walking into Discovery Cove.

I don't like taking my clothes off at the best of times (of which there aren't many unless it's in a dark room) but while I've been over here, I can't help but notice that in comparison I'm rather svelte. I've also noticed that over here, chubsters like me don't really care that much, hence the Victor's Secret

Well, why can't men have round 'em up / lift 'em up help to turn moobs into pecs?

Makes sense to me. And big spanks so we can hide our belly balconies? I quite like the idea of big Mickey Mouse shorts for blokes, ya know, the red ones with the buttons up the front? They look dead comfy - it looks to me like everything is tucked in where it should be, with no balcony or belly exposed whatsoever.

No wonder Mickey's always smiling.

Today was another crack of dawn start as we had Discovery Cove first thing and you've got to be there early as the Dolphins have their lunch break at 11.00. These late nights and early starts, along with the 20 odd thousand steps a day route march we're on, have taken toll on my old bones and I'm totally exhausted.

This hasn't been a holiday – it's been like an expensive boot camp. One where you're plied with food and drink, and then forced to perform adrenaline fuelled exercises whilst yomping across hot concrete.

I've decided I'm doing something just a touch more relaxing next year so I've booked a fortnight living in the Siberian Salt Mines, foraging for food and having my eyeballs scraped with a cheese grater.

Or Skibbereen, depending on the weather.

I can't moan too much as today was our last day, and my birthday. So, as a treat, Missus H booked us a day in a posh water park where you can swim with dolphins and sharks, snorkel with deadly manta rays and eat bacteria coated, lukewarm food off paper plates in your Speedos whilst watching fellow fatties spill out of flowery swimming cossies.

Sounds fun, uh?

It wasn't.

I do like Discovery Cove, especially in comparison to the other water parks like Typhoid Lagoon or Blister Beach. Disco Cove is way more relaxed – there's less kids, no loud music and no mad, steep slides with them plastic seams that rip apart your muffin tops.

But, what there is here, as there is in all water parks, is puddles of stagnant water.

Blurrrrggh.

I've just nearly been sick in my mouth...

I hate these puddles, especially the one's near the loos...

Bluuuurrrggghhhh...

Along with having to expose more than 35% of flesh, it's something that I really hate about water parks and I have no idea why it doesn't freak anyone else out. Horrible little collections of lukewarm, stagnant fluid, filled with other people's skin, toenails and god knows what else, waiting for you to tread in em without your flip flops on...

Blluuuuurrrggghhhhhhh...

I'm the same with that little collection of water you get in the bottom of the Dyson muffler type hand dryers. You know, that collection puddle full of bacteria that gets blasted over your fingers just after you've washed em?

Bbbbllllluuuurrrgghhhhhhhhhhhh...

I need to change the topic cos all I can think of is hairy corn plasters and it's putting me off my scratchings.

We were booked for a dolphin swim at 09.00 so turned up nice and early for our briefing in the Starfish Cabana where we were patronised by a very camp young man called Chipper "Chip" Buckley Jr. He thanked us for turning up and showed us an horrific video that we thought was the way sea creatures were caught but was actually behind the scenes footage of the chefs preparing the fish salad for lunch.

He then went on to explain that the small fortune we'd all paid to be here today has probably saved a whale from choking on a bin liner, and then proceeded to blame all of us for polluting the ocean in the first place.

He went through the rules of the dolphin swim (take off your jewellery, don't look the dolphin in the eye and definitely don't stick your fingers in the blowhole) and before you can say Moby Dick, I'm stood in 3 feet of dark cold water which is freezing my mummy daddy button, making clicking noises to make a grey fish flap its tail.

The most amazing thing was, however, that Missus H did it.

She doesn't like water. Or fish. Or dolphins. Or

getting her hair wet. Or being more than 12 feet away from a loo.

So, getting her to hang on to the fin of a big dolphin and being dragged 60 foot along the cove in deep water was some achievement I can tell you.

Not bad for £500.

The rest of the day passed in a bit of blur, thanks to the "free" booze on offer. In between power naps and going round the lazy, bird-infested river when I needed a wee (yeah, like YOU'VE never done it) I did my best Jack Cousteau impression in the big fishpond. This came abruptly to a halt when I swam right up to the shark tank and forgot there was glass in between – however, the trumps I let out provided extra speed as I darted off. Sort of like a fatman version of an outboard motor.

And so, after nearly an hour of washing salt out of my hair and disinfecting my left foot after I'd inadvertently stepped in a little kids' wee (Bllluuuurrrggghhhh...), we headed back to the pretend Italian Hotel and a very special date night for my birthday – a well-earned trip to Hooters.

Lads, let me tell you, it's ace.

Not just cos of the friendly, scantily clad, slim, nubile young girls with bright teeth, sunny dispositions and college degrees in cheerleading, but because of the food. The breasts are amazing! (I had sweet chilli and buffalo, and Missus H had the usual boneless platter).

But, I have to confess the charm didn't last long as it is a little intimidating for oldies like me, surrounded by young beautiful women. And not cos it's all fake teeth and tits and sprayed on suntans, or because they lost interest in our table after I'd asked if they accepted Disney Dingo Dining Credits instead of cash for a tip – it's because these women would never talk to a chubby middle-aged bloke like me in real life.

Which is a shame cos I was dying to ask Kokodamol-Staycee Colorado where she had her nails done.

In my youth, with a slim figure, sparkly eyes and a six pack, I'd have been the confident, cocky buck with loads to say to impress the likes of Layla-LeBronks, Patti DeChannelle or Katie-Boo Chuckamuffin.

(Why can't these girls just be called Karen. What's wrong with plain Anne or Pat?)

If we do try to chat, the perception is that we're weirdos or pervs or both. That's only partly true and sometimes it's just nice to have a chat to someone with big boobs.

No, what old gits like me want is something totally different to Hooters. Somewhere we're not intimidated by younger women and can just relax. Somewhere where the women serving us are of a certain age – old and wisely instead of young and happy.

Women called plain Margaret, Agnes or Hilda.

Where they have REAL bodies and aren't obsessed with cocking a hip to stick their butt out because they CAN'T cock their hip cos they've just had a new one put in.

Where they have as much lipstick on their teeth as they do on their lips.

Where they listen to you properly and tut in agreement when you moan about unexpected roadworks, the price of a pint or the cost of a bag of bark chippings.

Instead of young, fit girls, what we need is proper, real buxom, shapely women. Women who's bosoms are kept aloft by industrial strength bras and figures defined by Spanks. You know the type of woman with a chest that enters the room before she does, preceded by a heavenly cloud of Coco Mademoiselle.

So, sorry young Hooters ladies, you're not for me. Us manly men like real women.

I'm gonna open a bar called BUSTers.

Imagine it – loads of blokes gathered together in awkward, stony silence, sipping warm pints, glued to the big sports screens showing a 5 day drawn cricket test or an allotment special with Fred Dibnah.

There could be special guest entertainment from a man who's good at bleeding radiators, or someone that can do great impressions of a selection of creaking shed doors.

Better still, a singsong of Barry Manilow, Bing Crosby or Billy Joel hits.

We could have a cool merch stand selling everything BUSTers so the sozzled clients have got something to take back home for their loved ones after spending way too many hours being happy. Just off the top of my head we could have:

- BUSTers Buzz Off Facial Hair Removal Cream
- BUSTers Bone Soothing Hip n Knee Balm
- BUSTers Femicushion for Pelvic Floor Foundation

We could have an extra special range which includes portable fans that simultaneously blow hot and cold and stick-on patches that can be used to release soothing hemp extract or to just cover your husbands mouth.

The premium product in this range would be the Woman-Hood – imagine a bird of prey type hood that goes over the eyes and ears when you need to shut out the outside world. It would have a built-in neck fan and be made out of a jasmine scented, lush velour with tiny speakers pumping in the hits of Gary Barlow or Darren Day.

This is the best idea out of all the great ideas I've had in this book. I think it's a goer so I'm off now to apply for my liquor licence off Orlando Mayor, Buddy Duke Dyer.

If any of fellow Middle Aged Grumpies wanna invest, just let me know.

P.S. Too pissed to check the weather in Skib.

Travel home day

Sponsored by Wonga, for when you have no kidneys left to sell.

Our last night (my birthday) ended with us drinking way too much gin at Hooters, followed by alcoholic milkshake nightcaps in another womanly themed bar round the corner called, aptly, Twin Peaks.

Then three sachets of Gaviscon and half an hour lying completely still on the bed telling Missus H not to move me love, or I'll be sick.

And, if I did fall asleep, to roll me over on me side just in case.

Top night. Happy birthday me.

The next morning passed in a blur of dirty washing, stolen toiletries and strappy sandals as we shoehorned (literally, I nicked the shoehorn) everything into our bulging suitcases before heading to reception to pay the bill.

I'm gonna miss it here - the Portafino Bay is a cracking place to stay if Mr Barclaycard has given you a specially extended credit limit, you like plastic Italian memorabilia and don't mind your missus being letched at by swarthy waiters.

The good looking young kid at reception pretending to be Italian, Paulo Ntini Dexter-

Hoffenheimer Junior, looked scathingly at me and the pathetic state I was in. Knowing I had a hangover, he spoke deliberately **loud** and after making me promise I hadn't eaten the $15 Toblerone or the $10 mini Pringles, presented me with a settled bill.

Satisfied he'd dealt with me, good riddance, he then turned his horny attention to Missus H, asking if she'd had a nice stay, and checked to see if she needed any help with her luggage or adjusting her bra strap.

Well, that's what I think he said. Perv.

Before you can say "Luciano Pavarotti" we were headed to MCO and an ensuing few hours of total chaos. Another hurricane, Hurricane Dorian, was about to hit Florida so the airport was mega, MEGA busy.

A busy airport means two things to me – my anxiety level raises to 8 on the Scaredy Cat Flyer Richter Scale cos I'll get limited time for my vodka hunt and it massively increases the number of dumb people in the security queue trying to fly out before the wind blows all the planes off course.

MCO was full of em today. It was like a Stupid Convention. I haven't seen so many thick people since I spent a morning at a car boot sale in West Bromwich. I swear I saw one bloke trying to scan his fag packet barcode to get through the security barrier and heard another woman asking if she could Fast Pass the immigration queue.

Sorry to go on about this but what is it with these people who leave it til they get to the conveyor to open their bags up and spend the next 5 minutes ferreting around looking for laptops, liquids, pen knives...

Aaaarrrggghhhhhhh!!!

Look, it's dead simple...

To make it easier to get out, simply avoid putting your laptop in first, followed by a year's subscription to OK! Magazine, your spare phone charger, your portable rollers, yours and your cousins, uncles, mates house keys, the two books you'd promised to read but didn't / won't ever, the family pack of Caramel M & M's, a pile of receipts you were going to sort through, spare knickers cos ya never know at your age and the Sky remote.

Oh, and try not to look surprised when the security bloke tells you that you can't take on a litre bottle of Cilit Bang.

Anyroad, we eventually scuttled through security, that daft monorail and headed for the Posh Lounge so I could have another attempt to break the Guinness Book Of World Records for petty thieving of miniature sandwiches and muffins. I'd come prepared this time with a fold out Primark bag and Norris McSquirter on speed dial.

As I might have mentioned two or three hundred times, I don't like flying so to trick my brain into thinking that I'm actually going on a loooong train journey (I love trains, me) I need just the right amount of mind-bending booze. Settled into a chair far enough away so the staff won't see me making a pilfered picnic, Missus H and I became a shuttle run tag team getting single vodka shots to add to the Schnapple Apple juice I'd just bought from the convenient but terribly expensive airport shop downstairs.

The girl behind the bar, Grayysun-Maysee Chatanooga, cottoned on eventually but by that time we'd already filled two bottles, or 30,000 feet's worth, so we were good to go.

I was glad to leave to be honest - there's only so many pastrami n swiss sandwiches and macaroons you can eat before you have to be loaded on to the plane by hydraulic hoist in a bariatric chair.

Funnily enough, I used to go to school with a kid called Barry Atric.

Honest.

Greek lad, really good at football. I saw him a little while ago and he hadn't half put some weight on.

Missus H cajoled me down the airplane ramp as I simultaneously trumped and giggled, eventually reaching the door just as I started to sing "Hakuna Matata…"

With a concerned look, the ample bosomed, tight suited Virgin girl checked with Missus H to see if I was ok and, satisfied that I was no threat to anyone's safety other than my own, allowed us on the plane with a friendly warning that from now on I was her responsibility.

And that was that. Three weeks gone in a blink of an eye. At around 14.00, the wheels of the big plane left the tarmac of MCO and we headed home – goodbye America.

*****

Woosh, and in no time we were back in the Black Country and home to the kids and the dog. Molly was dead chuffed and she loved her Mickey Waffle. That 5 seconds that she played with it was well worth the $18.00 plus tax.

And I think the kids were happy we were back. I couldn't really tell as they'd gone feral and were speaking in a made-up language consisting of grunts, snorts and hand gestures. Luckily for us, they'd completely emptied the fridge so we didn't have to worry about food, and left us the washing up in case we were bored! Bonus!

Bloated from the plane and with jetlag and deep Disney blues, we started the dreaded task of unpacking to see what's leaked or broken this time.

The unpacking and stock take of Missus Hs strappy sandals was interrupted by a knock on the door, where I was met by a stranger asking if "that bag of stuff" was still for sale. My immediate concern was that while we were away the kids had turned our bedroom into a cannabis farm. Again. Turns out that they'd run out of money after week one and had resorted to selling my clothes on Used Dudley. (I do miss my "MC Hammer" drop crotch pants, but they did fetch a fiver).

Thanks for reading my stuff. Until the next time...

Grumpy out

Tara a bit

P.S.- The weather office in Skibbereen wrote to me and asked me to stop posting misleading weather reports. It was 25 degrees and sunny there at the time.

Interlude

Hope you enjoyed the first part. We're going to have a brief pause now before heading off to Paris for the final leg of this mammoth Intercontinental Adventure.

If this were a theatre, you'd be down at the front now, queuing for 2 small tubs of organic ice cream at £6 each from a Devon dairy you've never heard of.

I'll have a raspberry ripple, bab.

Although it will only take you a few minutes to read this, the actual length of time between flying home from Orlando and jetting off to Paris was 4 years.
4 long years!

Not much happened in that time. Well, apart from Donald Spunk Trumpet attempting to overthrow US democracy, Meghan Markle leading Harry by the hand to pastures new and Brexit.

Oh, and a worldwide pandemic that affected every nation on earth.

So not much really.

Since our trip to the Disneys in California and Orlando back in 2019, superbly covered in the first part of this book I have to say, a few things have changed at home.

The biggest one is that both kids have moved out.

Sam was the first to go – as I write he's just about to start a career as an airline pilot and lives with his utterly delightful and incredibly talented girlfriend Leah near Gatwick.

Then Lottie went… she qualified as a paramedic during Covid and grew up very quickly. One minute she's a nerdy 19-year-old, the next she's a hard nosed para, working on the front line during a worldwide pandemic. She met a bostin Black Country fella called James, also a top paramedic and a thoroughly good bloke. They fell in love and live together just around the corner – close enough to keep Missus H happy on a daily basis.

The other big change was the addition of two more cockapoos. Fearing the worst, we stuffed the child vacuum with two more dogs, bringing the total to three and outnumbering the humans. Rosie and Pip joined Molly - they were lockdown dogs and they are both equally delightful and annoying at the same time. More of them later.

The bell has just rung to signal the start of the second half. Hope it's better than the first… have I got time for a quick wee…?

So, there you have it. 4 years between the last trip and this next one so buckle up and enjoy.

Why Disneyland Paris, Michael?

Dear reader, before we head off to Paris for the final leg of this mammoth, multi-national Disney journey, let me transport you back to October 1992 and a town in the heart of the West Midlands called Brierley Hill.

Picture the scene – a dilapidated, former steel town in the heart of the Black Country. Decades of neglect, lack of investment and successive incompetent councils have turned a once thriving town famous for it's hard work and even harder folk into a shadow of its former self. The glory days of four banks (**four**- imagine that!), a thriving market, library and bus stops at <u>both</u> ends of the High Street to cater for the old ladies with those tartan shopping trollies are long gone, slowly replaced by an all too common sight in 90's Britain – boarded up windows, fast food joints and charity shops.

There's a whiff of despair about the town, only replaced by the heady smell of fat and pig skin when the bins are collected from the scratchings factory. The locals, known as Brierley Hillbillies, have long since given up hope of a better life and are resigned to being on the dole, smoking roll ups and drinking meths whilst watching Jerry Springer boxsets on stolen VCRs.

There was a brief beacon of hope when a new, ambitious young mayor tried to raise the profile by applying to twin the town with Walsall –

unfortunately they were already in advanced talks with Dudley so he had to settle for a suicide pact with West Bromwich.

But, in the middle of this bleak, industrial wasteland there was a true love story about to blossom, proving that even in the harshest of environments it's still possible to find romance and for a randy young bloke to get his leg over.

Oooh, went all 70's then...

One bright autumnal afternoon, a slim, bleached blonde haired young man wearing double denim and Deirdre Barlow glasses slowly drove his blue Toyota MR2 down the High Street heading for the stationers. (This is me, by the way). He'd just burnt up his last 80 kilobyte floppy disk copying an MS DOS file containing a massive 10 addresses so needed extra supplies.

As he inched forward in the traffic listening to Barry Manilow with the windows down, he saw a vision coming out of the fruit shop.

A vision in a tight, light blue nurse uniform. A vision with blonde curly hair, a vivacious smile and two large melons.

And behind her was Catherine.

I'm kidding, of course.

It was Catherine. Their eyes met for a brief second before the traffic started to clear and the MR2 roared the last 50 yards and screeched to a halt outside Brierley Hill Office Equipment.

Still in a daze about the size of the melons, our blonde hero stumbled out of the car and into the shop – not realising that right next door was the home of Dr. Phil Ing, the local dentist. Just as he entered the stationers, the sexy nurse waltzed past, smiled and headed into the surgery.

"Aaaah…" he said to himself with relief as he realised she's a <u>dental</u> nurse and not from the STI clinic or one of those tough ones from the Dudley funny farm.

As it happens, the owner of the stationers knew Catherine quite well, so he very kindly offered to be matchmaker. After a few days of apprehensive indecision, contact was made when the young buck (still me) sent a handwritten poem composed whilst on a sunbed after an aerobics class.

This is totally true, by the way.

And it worked.

She couldn't resist and in no time at all we were not only "going out" but pretty much inseparable.

And that's the way it's been for 30 years.

1 marriage, 2 kids, 3 dogs and three decades of love and happiness. All because of a traffic jam in Brierley Hill and a young guy's thirst for melons.

Our first holiday together was to France – we drove the same MR2 down to Dover, sailed over on a Brittany Ferry and spent a week cruising around until we ran out of traveller's cheques, conveniently right on the doorstep of what was then known as Euro Disney. A panicked call to my mum resulted in an emergency loan to Monsieur Disney which allowed us 2 nights in the newly built Sequoia Lodge.

I honestly can't recall any details about our stay, other than I know even then it was expensive, we were totally skint and pretty much couldn't afford to eat. I do remember being happy and excited to be in Disney without having to go on a plane (hate planes). I also remember that we had great fun together and laughed a lot – I found loads of photos since and we were both always smiling and very much in love.

Almost 30 years *to the day we first met*, we find ourselves back in the exact same place – only this time we have three nights booked in Sequoia Lodge and I can afford it with my own money so don't have to pay for it by cleaning my dad's Skoda Estelle for a year.

So, packed and almost ready for a few days of fun and nostalgia we made our last few preparations for our trip to Disneyland.

Ready?

Good. Let's go.

Allons-y!

Travel day / le jour du voyage

C'est notre tour!

(I promise not to litter the following chapters with poor French language gags otherwise it's going to become a bit of a cliché)

After the mad busiest year I think we've ever had which included 50th birthdays, new jobs, one kid moving house and another moving out, we found a short window of opportunity where we both had a few days to ourselves. So before Missus H could block book it with dog sitting, pottery making or house improvements I quickly booked a few nights to get our Disney fix with a little hop over the channel to Paris.

We picked Paris for a few reasons.

1) it was our 30th anniversary and coincided with 30 years of Disneyland Paris (see previous intro)

2) we couldn't afford Orlando.

Oh and…

3), despite my many, many letters to Walt he's still refusing to consider Disney Dudley.

I first wrote to him after our trip to Orlando in 2017. I explained that although he's got a great thing going on over in the US, what with the nice weather, great infrastructure and boppy waitresses and that, maybe he should consider building something a little easier to get to and colder for his British fans.

I may be a little biased here but Disney Dudley would be ideal. Not only has it got a great ring to it with fab alliteration, but the location and facilities we have are superb. It's smack bang in the middle of the country making it easy to get to for the southerners, scousers, Geordies et al and we already have a castle, a big zoo and a railway.

Well, a tram system.

On any Saturday night in every pub in Dudley there is an impromptu and very lifelike re-enactment of the famous Star Wars bar scene where all manner of alienlike creatures sup strange liquid and suck fruity vape from weird looking pipes as they listen to unearthly music, before one of em steps on another's handbag and they all start scrapping.

I must have written 20 times in the last few years with detailed plans, proposals, budgets and everything but he never wrote back. In fairness, I expect he's got a lot on his plate at the moment as he tweaks the business model to suit an ever-changing client base – for instance, he's trying to relaunch some of the Disney classics for the woke generation.

I'm told he's working on loads of follow ups, most notably The Perfectly Adequately Sized Merman, Robin Hood and His/ Her band of Merry / Miserable Nonbinaries and Snowflake White and the Seven Vertically Challenged Key Workers.

I'm not giving up though – just in the last few months as the Lottery money was dished out,

Dudley council have had a multi hundred-pound refit of the leisure centre including new toilets, a new-fangled swimming pool pump that filters out pubic hair a state-of-the-art vegan only vending machine. And we have 6 BRAND NEW traffic lights in the High Street. Wowzer.

Access is improving too - the HS2 route is only 20 miles away across 2 nature reserves, a rare newt pond and a pagan burial site so fingers crossed for when that gets built in 30 years' time.

This trip is just me and Missus H as both the kids are all grown up and have their own lives going on. Even if they had time and we offered to pay I don't think they would want to come. That makes me quite sad thinking about it but I don't blame them – they both think it's weird that a middle-aged married couple with no children in tow still burst in to tears on seeing a grown man dressed as a cowboy.

So we have 4 days to poke our nose around and see what Walts French cousin has created since we were last here.

Will it be as good as Orlando? Could it be BETTER than Orlando? Ya never know, maybe with a touch of Gallic flare and an extra portion of je ne sais quoi Monsieur Disney may have made it a little more sophisticated since we went in 1993.

Quite a lot has changed since the 90's – grown men go to work on skateboards and aren't considered weird, ballroom dancing is popular and the new rockstars are normal people who can bake fancy cakes.

I'm no longer a 28" waist, have grey hair and drive a van instead of a sports car. On the other hand, Catherine has aged incredibly well and still looks as amazing, sexy and vivacious now as she did back then.

I'm seriously punching folks.

To be honest, the trip didn't get off to a great start as in the process of planning (basically downloading the Disney App and having a scroll around) I discovered that my favourite ride ever, It's A Small World, is closed for refurbishment, thus denying me the opportunity to plant an earworm of the most delightful song ever. I know you're all gutted so I'll find out why and report back.

On a grey, damp Sunday morning the alarm went off at 05.15 and after much stretching, groaning and pumping we got ourselves in an upright position and I took my achy bones downstairs to make tea. Why is it so difficult to get up as you get old?

I'd packed the night before so didn't have that much to do, leaving time for last minute chores and flutters. For Missus H, this includes making sure the house is as secure as maximum-security prison. She has a set up that the old guvner of Alcatraz would have been proud of – cameras, deadbolts, security cameras... our house has more locks than Dudley canal.

A certain panic also sets in for Missus H during this last hour before we go away and all of a sudden she makes a start on meaningless jobs that have been put on hold for months. As I'm putting the cases in the car and making sure we have all the correct documents in order for the trip, she's decided this is the perfect time to rearrange all the cleaning stuff under the sink.

"Come on, we ay got time for that"

"It'll only take a minute. I've been meaning to do this for ages... You've got coffee on your shirt, idiot"

(I've always got some sort of spill on me and she's always the first to notice)

I go off to get changed as I hear her start up the leaf blower.

Eventually I wrangle Missus H into some sort of travelling companion and despite her attempts to just quickly creosote the fence we jump in the car headed for Birmingham Airport.

But not before we had said a long cuddly goodbye to our three pooches.

Meet Molly, Pip and Rosie. I know they sound like three characters from a 1980's BBC kids programme but in fact they are our 3 beautiful cockapoos. Named after Disney characters (extras in Lady And The Tramp - honest, look it up) they are the epicentre of Missus H's world. I knew we were both going to struggle with being empty nesters so it was no coincidence that they moved in just as the kids were moving out.

They provide a never-ending source of unconditional love and affection, entertainment and comfort. It's definitely helped both of us in such a major transition in our lives and is probably the one single reason that she hasn't knifed me.

We both got 4 days worth of snuffles in before we had to say goodbye. We put Molly in charge (she's the oldest and the only one who knows how to turn the heating down) and left them with instructions for the TV and just enough food to last til we're back..

Only kidding!!! We have an ace dog sitter called Margaret who looks after them when we're away. On Catherine's insistence and for an extra £20, she also dresses up as a security guard and can often be seen patrolling the house and garden, shining one of them big, long torches into the bushes looking for hidden ruffians.

So, with heavy hearts and even heavier suitcases, we sped off to catch an Air France flight to CDG.

Surprisingly, check in and airport security was an absolute doddle and we were through in no time at all, literally walking through the boarding pass scanner and straight in line to get our carry ons x rayed.

This lead me to believe that they must have put a Black Country person in charge since the summer debacle of massive queues and missed flights. No offence to my Birmingham cousins but as soon as you stick a high viz jacket on a Brummie and put him in front of a computer screen the power goes straight to his head and he turns into a Little Emperor.

There was a slight hold up as Missus H had to offload a monkey wrench, can of WD40 and a set of Allen keys (she was bleeding the radiators just before we left) but in no time we were skipping though duty free trying to avoid the caked up dollybirds attempting to spray 75 quid perfume at us.

"Katie Price Love Juice, madam?"

I'd booked us into a posh lounge as I do like a vodka or 6 to calm the nerves (as documented, I'm not good at flying) and also because it gives me an opportunity for petty pilfering of snacks that may come in handy later on. This amoral habit is something in my Black country DNA – don't get me wrong, I'm not advocating theft and I'm not that skint that I can't afford to buy a croissant, but I do get a real kick from pushing the limit on what I can have / get away with. I balance my conscience by accepting that:

a)   Man is a hunter gatherer and it's his duty to provide for his family (I realise this is a stretch... we're in Birmingham airport, not on the Serengeti)

b)   I'm saving the planet. I've already paid for these goodies and if I don't take em they'll end up in land fill.

Today's lounge was pretty well stocked with the added bonus of lax security so while Missus H was buying even more mascara in duty free, I waded in. I managed several tubs of honey (ya never know, I might get a sore throat) a few mini packets of Special K and an entire tray of flapjacks.

I'd give it an 8 out of 10 on the Pilfometer.

(The best lounge I've ever been in is the BA Executive lounge at Heathrow. My god that was good... pocket sized sandwiches, posh crisps and a well-stocked bar where you served yourself! It was a 10 on the Pilfometer but I deducted a point when they stopped the triple pack of posh biscuits and put cheap ones loose in a cookie jar).

Despite my nervous anxiety that the plane wings would drop off and both pilots would have simultaneous seizures, the flight was fine (well, what I can remember of it as I was smacked off my tits) and in no time at all we were through French security and battling through the drizzling rain to board a Magical Shuttle to Sequoia Lodge - our home for the next few days.

The shuttle wasn't like the Orlando ones. If you've been on them, you'll know that as soon as you're on board it instantly makes you feel like you're already in Disney with themed buses and loads of onboard screens welcoming you to the most Magical place on earth. This one had all the charm of a West Midlands bus replacement service from Smethwick to Wolverhampton.

It was packed with tired, wet families arrived from all over the continent, and even though I tried my best to get a singsong going of "It's A Small World After All..." we sat in damp, gloomy silence until we reached our destination.

We arrived at Sequoia Lodge to huge queues at reception and chaotic scenes in the foyer as multiple families were either checking in or checking out at the same time. I left Missus H to Candy Crush and watch the cases and went to stand in line.

After a little while, a cheery, friendly looking Disney girl came straight up to me to say hello and said, "Are you Michael?". Wow, I thought, she must recognise me from my Orlando books! Or maybe Monsieur Disney had advance warning of my arrival and had singled me out for "special treatment" in order to avoid any scathing criticism or my razor-sharp wit.

"Oui, c'est moi" I said in near perfect O level French. "Qu'est que c'est? Do vous know who I am?"

"No, your wife sent me over to tell you your flys are undone"

I hurriedly put the boys back in the barracks as I reached the desk.

I'd booked this hotel after more gin than research, so totally forgot that I'd ticked the upgrade option at checkout. This meant we were in a Forest Golden Garden room (I think that's what it's called) which not only meant that the room was a whole 3 square metres bigger than

241

most and you have a lake view but also that we got a few cheeky upgrades. The main bonus was access to the private Forest Golden Garden Lounge for a posh "All You Can Scoff" breakfast and again a couple of times later in the day – most notably for afternoon tea.

By a happy coincidence, afternoon tea was just about to start so I grabbed the room card and rushed up to the room. I unpacked while Missus H Crushed more Candy (she's a Grand Master) and in no time at all we were back downstairs heading for the Golden Forest Garden Lounge.

As mentioned, I do like to take advantage of any free snacks when presented with an opportunity... Well let me tell you that this lounge access opened up a whole new world of opportunities for petty pilfering.

All manner of French foodstuffs were on offer, beautifully arranged around a horseshoe shaped buffet. It ranged from big piles of tasty sandwiches to delicate patisseries. From fresh salads to moist carrot cake. From ice cold drinks to frothy coffees and pretty much everything in between.

There was even a mahoosive, wonderfully decorated, packed fruit bowl (I didn't nick anything from there - I'm not insane).

For a greedy bloke with a tendency to steal, this was Pilferers Paradise and scored neuf points from the Dudley jury.

We filled our boots.

Well, I did. Tinkerbell has a bigger stomach than Missus H and she gets full after a Hobnob.

I made a note to bring my big tote bag, Ziplocks and Tupperware for the following day and we headed over to the park for a quick fix of Disney Maqique.

*****

Sequoia Lodge is one of three impressive looking hotels right on the doorstep of Disneyland Paris. Along with its two sister hotels, Newport Bay Club and Hotel New York, they cover three sides of a huge, rectangular, man-made lake (unlike Orlando, not full of crocodiles) with an expansive boardwalk running around the periphery. On the fourth side of the lake is Disney Village, a small retail area with shops, bars and restaurants. Monsieur Disney has been very clever here... you can't get back to your hotel without walking through his shopping area, giving precious extra time to squeeze out your last few Euros on Disney tat.

We strolled slowly around the big lake as the sun started to set on a cool evening. That's when it really dawned on us that we were actually back in Disney – up until then it could have been any one of the hundreds of trips we've done together involving me drunk on a plane and checking in to a hotel.

We had a moment when we first saw the impressive Disneyland Hotel at the entrance and then blarted once inside when we heard the iconic Main Street music and set eyes on the castle. We're not soppy Disney nerds – it's just that this reminded us so much of the kids being little.

We had a slow bumble round and managed to walk straight on to a few rides in Discovery Land where I was roundly beaten by Missus H on the Buzz Lightyear spinnyshooty thing (she loves that ride) and took a trip on Star Tours (I love that ride). Tiredness and my desire for a cold beer started to creep in so we left well before the light show to avoid the rush and headed back through Disney Village for a €20 meal deal at McDonalds.

My beer fix was well and truly satisfied with a stop off at Billy Bobs Cowboy Tavern, a non-descript building with big, wide wooden staircases and two levels all looking down onto a central stage and dancefloor.

We grabbed a couple of pints and found a vantage spot on the balcony just in time to catch some amateur / comedy line dancing that not even the strongest pint of Belgian wheat beer could help us make sense of.

On the dancefloor were around 60 old people in cowboy hats and tassel shirts, loosely arranged in 6 rows of 10 each. On the stage were three very attractive lady instructors dressed as cowgirls who were evidently trying to teach these old uns how to move in time to a upbeat tune with a picky banjo.

They had their work cut out.

For a moment I thought I'd stumbled into a Texas old people's home at recreation hour. Or some sort of weird club for the rhythmically challenged.

As the pretty ladies on stage elegantly boot scooted one way then the other, hips swaying in time with the music, most of the folk on the floor seemed to be struggling with the basic concept of left and right, constantly turning into each other and falling over.

At one point I really thought that half of them were dancing to a different song.

One guy seemed to be freestyling away from the rows until I realised he was going for a piss and had a built-up shoe.

The tune came to an end just as an old guy in the middle attempted a jumping heel kick, almost wiping out an old biddy in a wheelchair dressed as Annie Oakley. They all yeehawed in self-congratulation – some even throwing their hats and zimmers in the air.

We decided we'd had enough fun and excitement for one day so headed back to the warmth of our room to do Wordle and get ready for tomorrow.

Bon nuit.

Le premier jour – matin

Despite my repeated requests (I call it prompting, some may call it nagging) the night before for Missus H to get up early enough for breakfast / Early Magic Hours AND bringing her a cup of tea in bed this morning we were still late leaving the room so we had to miss our "All You Can Scoff" breakfast in our private lounge before heading to the parks.

She likes to take her time in the morning does Missus H. Despite the fact we were going to miss breakfast, she still found time to prop herself up in bed drinking tea, whilst simultaneously Crushing Candy and checked her cameras.

Oooh, she does love her cameras.

At any given time, wherever she is in the world, she has total visual and satellite access to every corner of her universe, enabling her to keep track on the dogs, the kids and gawp at our young postman.

Our set up would be the envy of a small rural bank.

We have two Ring doorbells (we've only got one front door so one of these is propped up on a window sill, aimed into the lounge) an internal, multi direction camera trained on the kitchen that has an built-in microphone so she can talk to / scare the shit out of the dogs, and a separate set of 4 high resolution, motion sensor cameras which cover all aspects of our house, drive and garden. She switches between all sets of tech like a TV director, sometimes having all cameras lined up on her phone, tablet and even on her watch.

On top of that, she's put air tags in all of her handbags and the suitcase to make sure they can't get lost and constantly checks the whereabouts of both grown up kids on "Find My iPhone", renamed "Find My iNphant".

She's like Davros without the Dalek skirt.

She checked in with animals, kids and cases and satisfied that all planets in her universe were aligned, we wandered downstairs, outside and across the boulevard. Missing breakfast meant we made up some time, so we still arrived just before "rope drop" at Walt Disney Studios.

Studios is a much smaller park than the Magic Kingdom but contains some great rides and plenty of things to see and do. The main theme is Hollywood so there's loads of movie type stuff including backdrops to film sets, themed cafes and an old fashioned, art deco boulevard in an area called Production Courtyard. There's also Worlds of Pixar and the new Avengers Campus, with both having loads of interesting buildings, rides and character meet n greets.

As is the case with all Disney parks, it is spotlessly clean, well laid out and every corner and angle provide a fantastic backdrop for family photos. Today was going to be lovely – the sun was just coming out and even at 8.30 you could tell it was going to be a bright, beautiful autumnal day.

Even with the Early Magic Hour, we were still too late to get anywhere near the new Crush Coaster (themed on the quirky Turtle dude in Nemo) so instead headed straight to the Marvel bit.

Wow. It's dead good.

It's actually called Avengers Campus – a place where all the Marvel characters go to relax and regroup after a hard day fighting a constant stream of baddies intent on blowing up the world.

Within the Campus, there are a few places to eat protein based food for extra energy and a big Marvel shop with superhero priced tat, all surrounded by a cosmic world backdrop of buildings taken straight from any one of the film sets.

There are two mega rides – first off, we did the Avengers Meets Aerosmith coaster as there was no queue (I mean, literally no queue. Never happened to us before. We walked straight in as they were mopping the floor and at one point thought we'd walked into a staff canteen). This is the exact same ride as "Rock and Roller" in Orlando – you know the one where Aerosmith have been on a loop for twenty years and Steven Tyler's skin looks like a stretched ballbag. As we were first on, we got the front row so screamed all the way round as we were tossed from side to side and upside down. In hindsight, I'm glad we didn't have breakfast.

Avengers completed, we headed off quickly to get in line for the Spiderman thing. It was still nowhere near 9 o clock but the queue was already up to 45 minutes.

While waiting, we were entertained by a cute French kid dressed as a mish mash of his favourite Marvel characters. Captain America shield, Spiderman gloves and a string of Hulk snot dangling from his nose, he fought thin air baddies with swooshes and kicks. It came to abrupt and painful halt when he karate chopped a bin that he mistook for R2D2 and his mum rushed him off to get medical attention.

The ride itself is fabulous. The basic premise is that Peter Parker has created an army of asexual, self-procreating crabs to help him fight the baddies. At some point during production, he must have used a dodgy component from Maplins and now the naughty crabs have run amok in the big city, chewing and eating everything in sight.

With no training and zero risk assessment you have now been recruited to help destroy the zombie crabs and get him out of the shit with Tony Starc.

Donning 3D specs, you get strapped into a small spinning caravan and when it comes to a halt in front of a CGI screen, you use your wrists as weapons to zap crabs with a laser (there's a clinic in Dudley that does that).

It's fast and frantic and you're soon exhausted from using your new spider hands to shoot imaginary laser beams or flicking your wrist to chuck out a sticky web. It's a fab workout for the old Bingo Wings and thoroughly enjoyable.

Needless to say, I thrashed Missus H. She has great biceps and a good aim so was good at shooting the beams but I beat her at chucking out the sticky stuff as years of practice has given me a much better wrist action.

We emerged into bright sunshine to find the park was full of new superhero recruits and ride queuing times on the Disney app had gone through the roof. We decided to take a break in Marvel land, have a snack bar or two and do a bit of people watching.

I'm very glad we did.

In no time, a whole host of Marvel characters appeared before us, chatting and mingling with the crowds and posing for selfies. There was Iron Man, Captain America, The Wasp and a character I'd never heard of called Loki. I turned to Missus H to ask which film he was in to find she'd run off after spotting Thor surrounded by a group of schoolkids. She quickly round housed them out of the way to grab some selfies and get a good feel of his big hammer.

There were gasps and screams of delight as all attention was diverted to the rooftops to see Spiderman make an appearance, bouncing on to the scene with a series of leaps and bounds, twists and turns and a good old spin on the pommel horse.

This guy was seriously good. He interacted with the crowd and had all the kids screaming as he leapt effortlessly from one rooftop to another, never missing a beat. He'd be dead good at fixing aerials.

We'd all like a superpower wouldn't we? Like most blokes I'd like to make myself go invisible. Not for any pervy reasons, but just as it would be nice for no-one to know where I am so I could get a bit of peace and quiet.

Missus H has got a superpower – she can detect and pluck ear and nose hair with a lightning pincer movement, leaving her victim (me) stunned and shocked. She does this a lot, mainly on account that since I hit middle age my ears and nose have become miniature forests. She especially likes to do it on packed trains or in front of my mates. Sometimes she's less subtle, grabbing my chin and yanking my head towards the light saying "let me inspect ya dickhead. Urrrgggh, what's that?"

Regrettably, I've missed the boat with the Marvel franchise – I was never really into "superheroes" growing up as a kid. I much preferred the gritty, British humour of the Beano, Dandy and Jackie to the colourful, muscle-bound, made-up worlds of American comics. This all stopped of course, when I reached a certain age and the only thing I ever read was my mums Grattan catalogue.

Well...I say "read".

The Grattan catalogue was every horny young boy's dream.

I still remember that warm, fuzzy feeling that I experienced the first time I found my mum's 1972 Grattan catalogue lying open on the girdle page, a memory which, to this day, is the sole reason for my fascination with burlesque and why I get turned on by the trussed-up fishnet around a joint of beef.

You have to remember that in the 70's when sex was a taboo subject, there was no such thing as internet porn and the closest you ever got was looking through a stolen copy of your parents "Joy of Sex", fascinated by the sight of a gigantic bush of pubes and hairy armpits.

And the men weren't much better.

I may have been a little too obsessive as my mum suggested counselling when aged 14 I tried to enter Junior Mastermind with my specialist subject as "Playtex Pantyhose, Girdles and Corsets between pages 56 to 60".

Back to the Avengers Campus and now having spent some time here and seen pictures of Scarlett Johansson as Black Widow, I think I'll put them on my "Films to Watch" bucket list.

We ambled about a bit then finished the morning with a long, frustrating wait to get a coffee and croissant in one of the few concessions that was open. One thing that can't be Disneyfied is the French attitude to service and for a country that prides itself on good taste and cuisine they have a very strange habit of not wanting you to have anything.

I love France.

Love it.

Had more holidays in France than anywhere else in the world, with my parents and as a parent.

But Christ Almighty they don't half make it hard.

I don't wish to bring down the tone of the book as we're all having a laugh and a lovely time (I thought the Spiderman bit was particularly good, don't you?), but the staff working in these concessions need a Buzz l'Éclair rocket up their arse.

Anyway, the croissant was nice.

Le premier jour – après-midi

After a few hours over in Studios, we decided on a change of scenery so took the short walk across the boulevard to the Magic Kingdom.

It's a very pleasant walk, with colourful flower beds, cascading water features and bronze statues of Mickey and Minnie providing excellent photo opportunities just in front of the entrance.

Framing the approach to the park is the beautifully designed Disneyland Hotel, a pastel pink wooden shuttered Victorian style building. It's pure Disney, reminiscent of the Grand Floridian in Orlando, with tall turrets adding a nod to enchanted castles and a huge Mickey Mouse clock overlooking the new, excited customers about to enter his Magic Kingdom.

It's closed at the moment. Disney say it's for a top to bottom refurbishment, but rumour has it that there was a vermin infestation. How ironic.

We strolled down Main Street, dropping into some of the shops looking for gifts. I get that this park is nowhere near as big as Orlando and maybe the European Disney nerds aren't as thirsty for merch as their Humerican cousins, but there's nowhere near the same choice and variation to snaffle your Euros. And every shop is like the Scooby doo background.

I was rather hoping to find something new to add to my Grumpy collection but he's not as popular over here. Maybe French dads just aren't miserable bastards?

I really liked the look of the lycra Spiderwoman suit or the Princess Leia dressing up outfit for Missus H. I showed the girl some pictures on my phone, admittedly not from a Disney website, but she suggested I leave before she called security.

We had a wonderfully slow walk around Fantasyland, making our way there via my favourite ride, It's A Small World. I get it's not for everyone, but I love this ride – the magical set pieces representing each nation of the world, the quirky little dancing dolls dressed in traditional outfits and the enchanting music.

You're humming it now, aren't you?

How does it go again...?

After three.

One. Two. Three.

"It's a small world after all...

"It's a small world after all...

"It's a small world **aaaffter** all...

"It's a small, small world..."

You're welcome.

Unfortunately for me and its thousands of fans, it's currently closed for refurbishment.

It's a pitiful sight. It's surrounded by a security fence and the entrance where once you stepped through in excitement and wonder with a sign saying "Queue time 5 minutes" is now boarded up with a little notice saying it's fermed. Just in the distance you can still see the delightful, multi coloured façade through a small gap in the fence.

I ventured round the side, hoping to catch a glimpse of one of the golden gondolas, but all I could see was labourers tearing down England and chucking the Beefeater dolls in the skip. They seemed to be enjoying it a bit too much for my liking.

As I peered through the gap with tears in my eyes, I was met by a security guard who politely said I can't go any further. I bet he gets this all day, every day.

We struck up a conversation and in my best French asked him "Qu'est-ce que c'est going on ici monsieur?"

He explained that due to recent political events, the French government had seconded all the little boats and sent them to Calais. Apparently, they're in high demand there.

They had also made Monsieur Disney renovate the English set piece to better represent its place in the modern world. Instead of sweet little Beefeater dolls and Grenadier Guards in bearskins dancing in front of Tower Bridge, there will be a huddle of gender neutral, non-binary, expressionless figurines wearing rainbow backpacks who glue themselves together every 5 minutes, to protest at the unfairness of life and the government's refusal to acknowledge the rights of menwomen to recognise themselves as cardboard.

He said they're having trouble getting these new dolls to stay upright though as they have no backbone.

There will also be a special docking area where every third gondola will stop, unloading all male passengers and give them a free house, iPhones, spending money and a voucher to bring over unlimited members of their family.

To top it off, they are moving England right into the centre of the ride so it can be seen by all the other nations, creating an opportunity for each country to have at least one doll pointing at us and pissing themselves laughing.

Bit of political satire there... Might leave that bit in. Amazon will never check.

The Fantasyland bit is not really for a muddle-aged married couple with no kids, but it does provide loads of opportunities for us to practice our new hobby. As we're childless and free to do whatever we want, we have discovered something today – something that we've never experienced before at Disney.

Time.

Time to sit and watch in a Disney park. Time to take in our surroundings, watch what's unfolding in front of us, enjoy the spectacle and lunacy of a park filled with families having a great time and making memories.

We've never done this before. Every trip we seem to have done has been at a million miles an hour, pushed along by the sheer volume of people all trying to do the same thing as us, get on the same ride, queue for the same food.

We plonked ourselves on a bench near the Dumbo the Flying Elephant and stopped to watch.

Well, I did. Missus H had just completed the new level in Candy Crush and was now watching dog stuff on TikTok.

It was a happy scene with loads of princesses, some of them girls, waltzing around in their best frocks. Mums and dads were doing their thing – guiding their little ones, feeding them and wiping their chops.

One little boy was wandering around crying, eventually to be found by dad. Ironically, he'd just got lost in the queue for the maze.

I was just about to grab some popcorn as a couple of groomed, handsome dudes skipped past us.

"Aaah, aren't they a cute couple" I said to Missus H.

"You can't assume they're gay" she said, looking up from a compilation of howling dogs on TikTok to see two guys wearing matching his and his Disney t shirts, holding hands as they skipped on to the Dumbo ride.

"Oh. Fair enough"

We meandered slowly back out of the park, taking the decision again to leave before the light show folks started to arrive. We had heard it was crazy busy and spaces would be at a premium, so we promised ourselves we would be better prepared for it tomorrow.

We zipped back over to Studios and managed to grab two great seats for the Mickey Magic show (which was very good, highly recommend) before getting in line for the last Frozen show of the day - in French, this is called La Reine des Neiges (The Snow Queen).

By now you'd probably gathered that I like a bit of Disney and hopefully that I'm an upbeat, positive kind of guy. So with that in mind it's quite difficult to say this and I'm sorry for being negative but this was total and utter, 18 carat turd, rubbish.

They have somehow managed to create an homage to Frozen that's baffling, short on humour, and misses most of the good bits out.

To add insult to injury, it's performed on two different stages by the same three actors (4 if you include Sven the reindeer and 5 if you include a CGI version of Olaf) and halfway through the performance they pause the show and get the audience to move into another part of the building!

I'm sure she's a sweetie in real life but the girl playing Elsa had a voice like a panicked goose.

It's merde.

If I were in charge, I'd close that down immediatement and make them come up with a better idea or replace it with something old school like Honey I Shrunk The Audience or Captain EO.

Oooh, that's a good shout. The King of Pop was quite big in France so surely Monsieur Disney has some old Michael Jackson memorabilia knocking about that he could fashion a kids ride out of.

Tired and weary with sore feet, we headed back through Disney Village and got in line for some food at the Rainforest Café. We like it here and in no time a chirpy waitress took us to our table underneath a grumbling gorilla where we scoffed pasta and sank a few well-earned beers before heading back to the room.

Le deuxieme jour – matin

I'd deliberately set the clocks back an hour to make sure Missus H was ready in time today as I'm convinced she's inventing new ways to slow me down first thing in the morning.

(Dons tin hat)

Are all women like this?

She's a genius at it. I'm always awake first on holiday and I can be up and out in 15 minutes – 25 minutes if I have to do my hair and strim my nose forest. Conversely, Missus H loves nothing more than a lie in, preferably in a dark bedroom with a cup of tea delicately placed by the side of the bed and just after I've wiped the sleep dribble from her chin.

When I do eventually get her vertical, she then becomes a moody teenager and has a full repertoire of routines to stretch out getting ready.

The "I've Just Got to Put Me Eyes On" routine
The "Hair up / Hair Down?" routine.
The "Does This Jacket Go With This Scarf?" routine
The "Which Shoes Look Best with These Jeans?" routine
The "Oh It All Looks Wrong!" routine (this is the one that I dread as it means the whole process has to start again)

This is on top of checking cameras, speaking to the dogs and completing a new level on Candy Crush and while I'm pacing the room trying not to swear.

I hinted at a 7.45 departure today as I thought it would give us plenty of time - at ten to 8 she's still stood in bra and knickers, curling wand in one black gloved hand and TikTok in the other whilst watching BBC news.

I mumble something along the lines of "Gonna miss breakfast now" or "We'll never make it to Crush at rope drop..." or "There's a meet and greet with Captain Thor first thing..." to try and hurry her along but to no avail.

I've learned to live with it. Next time I'm going turn the clocks back 2 hours.

(Removes tin hat)

I actually think that all women are great and not strange at all.

I chivvied her along just enough to avoid a kick in the shins and after a quick breakfast and giving her a piggy back around the lake, by exactly 08.35 we were in the queue for the new Crush ride with just a 45-minute wait.

Like most new stuff that opens, there's always a huge amount of hype, fuelled in no small part by the many Facebook groups and Disney forums, so we were excited to catch the East Australian Current and see for ourselves.

It's OK.

You're strapped in to a 2-seater clam shell, hoiked up a slope then catapulted along an indoor track in the dark, whizzing, spinning and gliding to mimic cruising through the EAC like a turtle.

I've actually made it sound better than it is.

It's a bit like the Wild Mouse ride at Blackpool Pleasure Beach but in the dark and without the smell of chips and despair.

Next off we darted over to Ratatouille. I really love this ride. It's another 3D jobbie and you're Remy, the star rat in the film. You sit in a small rodent shaped vehicle as it scuttles and scurries around the fat French bloke's kitchen, darting under cupboards and sneaking through cracks in the wall, all the time trying to avoid being squashed to death / poisoned by a collection of big nosed waiters.

Little known fact - the inspiration for this ride was an actual a real-life curry restaurant in Dudley called The Red Balloon Knot. Apparently, a top Disney exec was eating there the very night it was raided by environmental health and got closed for a vermin infestation. That's true! (*)

As usual, there's a shop at the ride exit and never one to miss an opportunity, Monsieur Disney has upcycled the rats he's caught from the

Disneyland Hotel and for just €25 kids can have their very own Remy! **

We sat awhile in the French bit of Ratatouille, having another one of those moments where we watched the world go by. It would have been perfect with a coffee and croissant, and I spotted an opportunity to get served in less than 40 minutes so got in line at one of the pop-up food stalls.

I'd love to know how Disney screen and interview these muppets that work the kiosks. This particular bloke was slow, arrogant and rude, with unkempt hair, scruffy appearance and a face that would scare a police horse. He looked the kind of bloke that eats roadkill.

As the queue built up, he slowed down. You could almost make out his inner monologue as he looked at the growing line of thirsty customers...

"Zey wan coffee...? Fuck zem..."

That's why the French eat snails – it's the only thing they can catch.

As it's pretend "Paris" there's also a massive smoking area which was packed with folks puffing on Gauloises.

Blimey, the French still love a fag don't they?

Apparently on the French version of the Disney app you get waiting times for the smoking areas and if it's really busy you can pay an extra €15.00 for a Fast Pass. Monsieur Disney knows his crowd so inside the smoking area there's a kiosk in the shape of a fag packet selling Mickey n Minnie rolling papers, Aladdin tip filters and a special edition Cruella de Vil ciggy holder.

As all the customers were French the service was rapid and there was no queue. Funny that.

We headed over to the Pixar Playland, a truly wonderful little corner of the park that has the look and feel like you're in a toddlers back garden, with playthings abandoned in the grass and a handful of rides dotted around the place.

It's delightful.

We drank in the sound of the Pixar music playing through the speakers, almost drowned out by the happy squeaks of excited children.

Just like we did when our kids were little, we slumped up a corner by some dominoes with a glass of red wine each. We stayed quite a while, taking it all in and watching all the beautiful little families having the time of their lives. It was a very melancholy moment and we were both fighting tears when we heard the first few bars of "You've Got A Friend In Me". Our kids grew up on the Pixar films and were both emotional wrecks when we hear anything by Randy Newman.

Our boy Sam is Toy Story and Lottie is Nemo. I'm crying thinking about it.

They're both all grown up now and moved away.

But I'd give anything, absolutely anything, for them to be little again. Just for five minutes.

To smell their hair after a bath, tickle them or let them fall asleep in my arms.

If you're reading this and you have little ones, give them an extra big squeeze next time as it goes so fast. Soak up every precious moment.

But there is a flip side... (parents are gonna hate this next bit).

Full of emotion and tipsy on booze, we wandered slowly back to our cozy room, took off our trainers, got our comfies on and had a 90-minute snooze.

Imagine that young parents. A red wine fuelled snooze in the middle of a Disney day.

Heaven.

(*it's not true)

(** that's not true either)

Le deuxieme jour – après midi

Refreshed from our snooze, we got ourselves battle ready for the evening park session and light show then made our way around the lake and into the Magic Kingdom for a late lunch.

We had a slight delay getting in as a scruffy looking 8 strong family all simultaneously queued and talked on the phone (they all had different phones… like, one each. They weren't on one gigantic phone).

The lead member of their party, the lady at the back (obviously) had all the tickets on her phone but she sure didn't let that minor inconvenience stop her from rabbiting on, despite the queue building up behind her. In fact, as she got near the scanner she seemed to revel in the fact that people were shouting at her to get off her phone, at one point turning to the crowd as asking them to shush as she couldn't hear!

I'm fairly sure if this was Alton Towers she'd have been lynched, or worse still made to watch a box set of Mrs Browns Boys.

Eventually we passed through the scanners just as the iconic Disney Railroad steam train pulled in Main Street Station. As a former trainspotter (no surprise there) I do love a steam train so we hopped up to the platform and jumped on just as the pretend conductor yelled "all aboard!".

We weren't on 5 minutes before we hit a bit of trouble.

There was a picket line at Frontierland Station and it turns out that the rail staff have gone out on strike just like their British cousins, demanding a pay rise above inflation, better working conditions and first dibs on character meet and greets.

We were forced to get off by a scouse shop steward and get a replacement bus service to Adventureland.

On our travels yesterday we'd spotted a Tex Mex fast food joint and luckily that wasn't too far away so headed across for some spicy food. Missus H is off meat at the moment so we both went for the vegan burrito meal deal. Packed with rice, beans and guacamole it's both **tasty** and good value – I'd highly recommend.

But be aware of the inevitable consequences a few hours later. Stood in a packed vantage point for the lightshow, I let out a pump so violent it parted a small child's hair.

Sat in the late afternoon sunshine with a fantastic vantage point, we people watched as we munched away.

Missus H is a fully fledged Podiatrist (she gave up the dental stuff and moved her medical attention to feet. I'm just glad she didn't stop halfway down and become a Bumologist) and her pet hate is folk, usually women, that wear the most inappropriate footwear for a long park day.

She wants me to tell you that her advice is to be sensible and always wear comfy shoes or trainers. Avoid high heels (I made that mistake the first day), those big clod hopper shoes straight from a Mr Man book and anything that hasn't got good arch and heel support.

There was a lady who sat at the next table with two hyper toddlers and a scruffy husband and she was wearing flat, open toed sandals that looked like they were made of cardboard. Offering no support or comfort at all, they were one puddle away from papier mache. She may well have strapped Weetabix to her feet.

We bimbled around Adventureland for an hour or so, catching the pirate boat as we sailed around the Caribbean and had a pointless mooch around the Swiss Family Robinson tree (is it me or is that just the most pointless thing ever in Disney? I don't get it at all... that sort of shite should be reserved for Go Ape).

As we left Adventureland we caught sight of Captain Jack Sparrow doing a meet n greet with some very excited young pirates so cruised over to have a look. This bloke sounded a bit like him and muttered in English and French but looked more like Captain Caveman. I can only assume he'd been drafted in at the very last minute – maybe the real pretend Jack had food poisoning from too many whelks. Even Missus H wasn't impressed and she LOVES Captain Jack. She especially liked him in that recent court drama when he played the part of Jonny Depp and had to defend himself against accusations of being a bully and his ex-wife did a poo in his bed. Seems a bit far fetched to me that storyline.

It was getting time to make our way over to Main Street so we could get a spot to watch the light show. Walking through Fantasyland as the sun started to go down was quite something, with the pink sky throwing more magic on to the castle. Folks stopped to get the perfect picture, battling for everyone to keep still and smile as their kids' batteries began to run out. It had been a long day for lots of these families and by now the little ones had had enough, no matter how hard their parents tried.

It's quite nice to watch other families doing their thing with little ones, even when they're all tired an grumpy, knowing that was us once. We put in the hard work for our kids back in the day and although it was frustratingly, annoyingly expensive and sometimes extremely challenging, we wouldn't have changed a thing.

If this is you now, stick with it – it's all worth it.

I wanted to see "La Taniere du Dragon" (the castle dragon) so we went down to the side of the castle, following the crowd into the gloom as the low growls and grumbles. Poor thing is chained up in a dingy cave and the as it woke from his slumbers the grumbling got louder and louder. To be fair I'd be like that if I was trying to sleep and I had French kids poking me.

It was very, very dark down there and, like most men who are still basically little boys, I am never one to miss an opportunity.

As I have done many, many times in the 30 years that we've been together, I reached down in the dark for a naughty bum squeeze. I felt a round, soft, delicious buttock and gave it a little cheeky pinch.

That's when I realised that Missus H was standing 15 feet away talking to the dogs on camera.

I turned round to see I'd now made a new friend - a smiling, cute German guy with a Dumbo Loungefly backpack, fabulous mascara and an outrageous jumpsuit called Hans Frei.

I apologised profusely as we swapped numbers and scuttled back to Missus H, just as she was cooing into her phone, trying to teach new tricks to three bemused dogs who can't see her, probably don't know she's been gone three days and think she's still upstairs putting on her make up.

I blew a kiss to Hans and skipped away. I'd like to think he'll remember me...

*****

Despite the fact we had to make do with a shit viewing spot by a bin, behind a tree and surrounded by the biggest French geezers in the park, the light show was amazing and made me realise why Monsieur Disney has to charge me €5 for a coke.

It kicks off with a massive "30 Celebration" display, with hundreds of neon drones above and behind the castle as the music builds to a crescendo. This is followed by the most amazing light show, immaculately cast on to the castle with all your favourite characters taking turns to sing their beautiful songs and stir up your emotions.

We were already blubbering wrecks – we'd had a great time, this was our last night and here we were standing holding hands in pretty much the same spot we stood as lovestruck youngsters nearly 30 years ago.

Then the "Up" balloons appeared and we both lost it, crying like a big pair of titty babbies.

We hadn't cried this much since we got our last electric bill.

It doesn't matter how old you get, Disney always find a way to tug at your heartstrings.

If Toy Story and Nemo are for our little kids, then "Up" is mine and Catherine's. The music to the opening sequence, followed by the storyboard life of Carl and Ellie is almost too painful for us to watch and a reminder that life is both precious and short. I know it's a film and I know they aren't real characters. But they loved each other very much and one day became apart. It will happen to all of us.

If you have a loved one in your life, go give them a hug now. Be like Carl and Ellie.

Drowned in emotion and on a promise, we ended the night by skipping food and getting absolutely plastered on the most expensive bottle of rose

I've ever bought and several "30 Celebration" cocktails in the hotel bar.

What a day.

Le dernier jour

We both woke up with stonking hangovers due to the killer combination of huge quantities of very expensive alcohol and a total lack of will power. In the middle of getting intoxicated, we had excitedly made mega plans for getting up early to pack, have a last breakfast and to be at the scanners at 8.30, in time for Early Magic Hours.

As we giggled and stumbled drunkenly into bed at 1 am, we both knew that was never gonna happen.

Today is our last day so after much stretching, parping and paracetamol I made Missus H a cup of tea (she's barely human before tea, never mind with a hangover) and with my brain bouncing inside my skull, I vowed never EVER, EVER to drink again and started the packing.

I do all the packing and unpacking, always have done. It's my thing.

(Roll, don't fold by the way. You'd be amazed).

I like to get organised before a big park day and so I always put different outfits on the bed the night before, depending on my mood, hairstyle, and the weather.

I've sort of become the human equivalent of a chubby, middle-aged Ken doll.

As we're on the continent and I really want to fit in on my last big day, I'd plumped for my lime green Pierre Cardin shirt, candy stripe blue and white culottes, and dusty pink espadrilles. I topped off my outfit by throwing an orange cashmere jumper around my shoulders, tied at the chest, and a beret.

I did think about wearing my electric blue chiffon neck scarf, but I think that would have made me look ridiculous.

One big difference we've noticed with the folks here versus Orlando is the very eclectic collection of cultures and fashion due to the multitude of stylish Europeans in the park.

In Orlando there's a sort of Identikit fashion- lots of board shorts, t shirts and baseball caps for the blokes and comfy, sporty gear for the ladies. Or whatever latest invention you lovely ladies think prevents chub rub.

Over here there are far fewer mirrors so it's very much laissez-faire with no norms at all.

The Disneyland Paris special edition of "Guess Who" would last forever.

"Has your man got an Hercule Poirot moustache, a top knot and a nose ring?"

"Has your lady got pink cornrows, ear stretchers and a pipe?"

"Has your man got a pudding bowl haircut, a goatee and Willy Wonka sunglasses?"

Bedecked in my very best European attire and with an extra splash of special edition Bon Maman "après-rasage", I whispered politely for

Missus H to take her head out of the pillowcase and become vertical.

After just an hour to chuck on the chop slop and do her hair, she checked the cameras one last time to make sure the house was still there, was still occupied by three yampy dogs and neither of the kids' phone was showing the location of an A & E department, she declared herself good to go.

We said goodbye to the room (we always do that, rooms have feelings) and checked out.

We had a few hours to kill before we caught the Magic Shuttle back to the airport so decided to spend the last few hours of our trip nursing the hangovers in our 2 favourite spots in Studios - the French Ratatouille bit and Pixar Playland.

As we'd missed the chance of the EMH, there was a long, 45 minute queue for Ratatouille so I had a "fuck it, I'm on my holidays" moment and forked out €25 for a couple of cheeky Fast Passes. I don't do stuff like that very often but as a one off it's worth it just to see the faces of the folk in the normal queue as they see you waltz straight down to the front. It's sort of payback for the coffee queue.

We giggled as we scurried around the fat Frenchman's kitchen and emerged into the sunshine feeling slightly more human.

We needed some sustenance to soak up the booze and luckily Disney had managed to drag some untrained layabouts out of bed and into work to man the food stations.

There's quite a few kiosks dotted about the place, mimicking street vendors in a village market, all selling tasty morsels and titbits from different parts of Europe. Most European nations are covered so you can get a small plate of tapas from Spain, olives and wine from Italy and greasy sausages and sauerkraut from Germany.

Notably, there isn't any British food so no opportunity for a kebab, chow mein or chicken tikka masala. I think a Black Country kiosk would go down a storm here... can you imagine the queue as the French discover faggots and peas with a side order of scratchings? Yummy.

I managed to grab something before the queues built up which gave Missus H the chance to check in on the dogs. When I returned, she was sobbing away, tears streaming down her cheeks.

"Blimey, you ok?"

"Yeah, I've just heard Pip fart in her sleep and it's made me want to go home... bllaaarrrr..."

I calmed her down with a promise to buy extra Bonios when we got back and then sat for ages in a perfect spot in pretend Paris, lapping up the autumn sun whilst sipping our coffee and watching the world drift by.

Fair play to Monsieur Disney on this one - he's got pretend Paris spot on. The buildings look real, the attention to detail is on point and the piped accordion makes you feel you could actually be in the Montmarte but without the graffiti and the smell of sewers.

For the last hour of our mini holiday we went back to Pixar Playland as we hadn't cried enough. I bought us a couple of glasses of rosé to toast what has been a fabulous few days and we meandered past the Slinky Dog ZigZag Spin and the RC Racer ride before finding a bench by the Toy soldiers Parachute Drop.

Fuelled by the booze and emotional as we were heading home, we both blarted as various theme tunes were played over the speakers and dressed up kids played around in the beautiful sunshine, pretending to be like their hero Buzz, Woody or Jessie.

God, I miss my kids when they were little.

We had a teary, emotional chat about the future, and how we both hoped be back here soon as grandparents.

The conversation turned to Disney and what it means to us - about how it's been a backdrop to our lives and the Pixar songs a soundtrack to the kids growing up.

Disney is totally unique - it brings smiles to faces young and old and makes lifelong memories to be cherished across generations. It's also inclusive, a safe space for minorities and really cares about giving access and support to families with special needs.

I turned to Missus H with tears in my eyes and choking back the emotion blubbered:

"Can you think of anywhere, *anywhere*, else on this planet where you would see more happy people altogether in one place?"

She stopped to think for a second.

Then said:

"Yeah. Crufts"

Thanks for reading.

Fin

Afterword

It's quite a lonely business, this writing lark.

Every word, sentence and paragraph of this book, and the 2 that preceded it, were invented, imagined and converted on to paper by me as I sat alone in the kitchen. Thousands of hours spent making notes, thinking of funny lines, trying to find an angle to get a message across and be entertaining at the same time.

Jesus, it's exhausting.

But I wrote this book because I wanted to.

I don't have an agent; I don't have a publisher. I'm never going to make any money from this - in fact I will almost certainly lose money as I must buy my own books up front in the hope that they will sell.

And even if they do, I'm giving the money away.

I wrote it because it means something to me. I want these events and moments in my life to be committed to memory - to place on record what happened and how lucky I was to share these experiences and stories with my loved ones.

I also want it to be a record of happy times with my family so future Hadleys can have a glimpse into the life that came before them.

Most of all I want my family to be proud of me for telling the world how much I love them.

If you have read this far, then you are a true friend. We may have never met, but we have a unique connection in that my words and thoughts have been absorbed into your brain. I am forever grateful and humbled - it means more to me than you can ever know.

Oh, and you paid for the book so some of your cash has gone to charity. Cheers.

I'm signing off now, but I can't go without paying tribute to my long-suffering travel and life companion... my Cloudbusting Lionheart, Catherine.

With no shadow of doubt, she's the best thing that ever happened to me and my sorry self and is the single reason why I'm still in one piece and not living rough on the streets of Dudley.

Catherine provides the calm to my storm. She keeps me safe when I'm in danger and provides cover for me when I'm being attacked.

She's my Puncture Repair.

She's funny, sexy, clever, talented... She is the most amazing wife, incredible mother and a true friend. Her fierce loyalty to me and the kids has been the glue that has kept us as a family together through many testing times.

As a medical professional, she has compassion, an instinctive, caring nature and provides comfort for everyone around her. A nurse in the very true sense of the word. She's adored by all of her wonky footed patients, especially the pervy old blokes, and for very good reason.

She is blessed with a kind heart and is loved by everyone who has the pleasure of being in her company.

To borrow a line, she is "the only thing in any room she's ever in..." (© Guy Garvey)

If God despatches angels to guard and guide us stupid men through our brief time on earth, I'm lucky, beyond lucky, that he chose Catherine to steer me through my life.

And that's the real reason I wanted to write this book. It's a bonus if it's made you laugh, and brilliant if it's raised money for charity. But best of all, it's a permanent record of happy times and a lasting tribute to my beautiful wife.

You never know, it might get me a handjob.

Printed in Great Britain
by Amazon